Birthday parties can be deadly . . .

Edging nearer, Leslie's heartbeat quickened. She wanted to turn back. Escape the funeral. But her feet dragged her forward. Closer to the coffin.

A body jerked up suddenly. "Granny!" Leslie cried.

Granny Barrows wore the same green dress she'd worn to her eightieth birthday party, and her green eyes sparkled brightly. Deathly pale, she radiated energy. Her eyes drilled into Leslie's. She stared right at her. Right through her. Then she pointed one gnarled old finger.

"Be careful," Granny warned, her voice quavering. "Birthday parties can be deadly."

Other Scholastic thrillers you will enjoy:

SWEET SIXTEEN

FRANCESCA JEFFRIES

SCHOLASTIC INC.
New York Toronto London Auckland Sydney

ISBN 0-590-67449-8

12 11 10 9 8 7 6 5 4 3 2   7 8 9/9 0 1/0

Printed in the U.S.A.   01

First Scholastic printing, September 1996

PART ONE

May 8, 1993
Saturday Night

Chapter 1

It was a strange night for early May. The temperature had climbed to 93 early in the day, and as evening fell it showed no sign of dropping. The air felt heavy, humid, and it pressed in close as Leslie Barrows sniffed the air.

It smells like rain, she thought. Like a storm gearing up for a full-blown attack.

Thunder rumbled in the distance.

This type of weather usually didn't hit Medvale until July, sometimes not at all. But here it was, barely even May, and a heavy listless feeling had settled around the New England town. People lined up at air-conditioned movie theaters. They strolled through cool, crowded malls. Baseball fields stood empty, and the hiking trails of nearby Mount Porter were deserted. It was too hot for any kind of exercise.

Leslie pushed her thick red hair away from her face. Sighing, she turned on the overhead fan in the kitchen, then went back to arranging crackers on a tray. What a night for a party, she thought. What a night for a birthday.

"Make that two birthdays," she reminded herself.

Leslie and her grandmother shared the same birthday, May 11. Today was the eighth, a few days earlier, but it was Saturday night, and the Barrows were getting ready for the party. Leslie would be turning thirteen, her grandmother eighty, and ever since Leslie could remember they had celebrated together, with double parties, double dinners, double everything.

For the first time, though, tonight's party was strictly a grown-up affair to honor her grandmother. Leslie's celebration would come the day of her birthday, with a fancy nighttime picnic after school. If, Leslie thought, crossing her fingers, we're not rained out. Thunderstorms had been predicted all week.

"Leslie, honey," her mother called from the living room. "How are you coming with those crackers?"

"Fine, Mom."

Carrying the crackers into the living room, Leslie threw a quick smile at her mother as she placed the tray next to a cheese board. Then she stooped to kiss her grandmother, who sat in the center of the room, her back erect, her expression distant. She rested her cool green eyes on Leslie, and suddenly her expression softened.

Granny was the uncontested head of their family. Everyone respected her. More than respected her, really. They held her in a kind of awe. Family stories and legends all revolved around Granny, how she had bravely journeyed to the United States from Eastern Europe by herself. How she had carved a brand-new life in a strange new land.

Granny lifted her left hand and her sparkling emerald ring flashed like lightning.

"Leslie," she said quietly. "You look lovely."

"And you look gorgeous," Leslie whispered.

Her grandmother smiled, dropping her hand on Leslie's. "You are as sweet as you look, child. You always have been."

Leslie's red hair fell in gentle waves around her heart-shaped face. Her green eyes had a brightness, almost a shimmer, and her nose was long and straight. People said she looked just like Granny Barrows, and at times Leslie could see it, too. Granny's hair had thinned over the years and turned a cottony shade of white. But her eyes hadn't dulled. And as she focused on Leslie now, they glowed with the force of pure love.

Leslie knew she and Granny shared a special bond. A connection. No one else in the Barrows family — including Leslie's older sister, Sharon — received this special look. And Leslie couldn't help but feel . . . What was the word? she wondered. Proud? Special?

Lucky?

The doorbell rang, breaking Leslie's reverie. The first guests were arriving. Quickly, Leslie ducked back into the kitchen.

"Happy birthday, Sophie," someone shouted loudly. "How does it feel to be eighty years old?"

"And how does it feel to be thirteen? Well, almost thirteen." Leslie's Aunt May strode into the kichen. Her daughter, Leslie's cousin Trisha, walked in behind her.

"What a night for a party," Aunt May chattered on. "It feels like the middle of an August heat wave." Smiling, she reached over and hugged Leslie. "You know, you're looking more and more like Granny every day. It's just so spooky you two have the same birthday, too."

Trisha had been poking around a cabinet. Now she slammed the door with a soft bang.

"Mom." Her voice was low, almost a whisper. "My thirteenth birthday's just a few weeks away. Does anyone remember that?"

"I remember," Leslie said. But Trisha stood with her back to her, rigid and tense. Leslie wasn't sure she'd even heard, but she didn't say anything else. She'd never been sure how Trisha would react to things.

Leslie sighed, thinking once again how nice it would be if they could be friends. Real friends. The cousins went to the same school, and sometimes found themselves in the same classes. And they were so close in age . . . lived so near each other. . . .

Trisha's face brightened suddenly with a hopeful look. "Mom," she began. "You know what I'd like for my birthday? A beautiful green — "

But Aunt May had already disappeared into the party, not hearing a word her daughter said. Trisha slumped in a chair. "So what are the birthday plans, anyway?" Leslie asked. She didn't want Trisha to feel ignored. "They should be big, for our first year as teenagers."

"Knock, knock!" A loud, cheery voice interrupted from outside. Trisha jumped up to open the back door, and Leslie's new neighbors, Mr. and Mrs. Shaw and their daughter, Deborah, stepped into the hot, humid kitchen. The Shaws were new to Medvale, and Leslie's mother had invited them to meet their neighbors. She'd included Deborah because she was the same age as Leslie.

"The front hall was packed, so we thought we'd sneak in this way," Mrs. Shaw explained. She hooked her arm through Mr. Shaw's and gently pushed Deborah toward Leslie. "Now stay with these nice young girls," she said, enunciating each word as if she were talking to a child. "Your dad and I are going to brave the crowds!"

Alone, the three girls stood awkwardly in the kitchen.

Deborah hung back shyly, twisting a strand of hair around her finger as she edged closer to the living room.

Finally, Trisha lifted her head out of the refrigerator. "You know, just because we're the same age doesn't mean we all have to hang out together."

Trisha's tone was almost conversational. But Deborah flushed, and Leslie, shooting a look at Trisha, waved her into a chair. "Don't mind Trisha," she said cheerfully. The words spilled out without her even thinking. "Of course we should stick together."

Deborah smiled gratefully. "You know," she began. "I really . . ."

Just then angry whispers floated into the

kitchen. Leslie knew the voices belonged to Aunt May and Uncle Fred, Trisha's parents. She couldn't make out what they were saying, but they were clearly arguing — again.

Trisha's face whitened. As the voices grew louder, she snapped a cracker in two.

"You can do whatever you want," Aunt May shouted. "No one's holding a gun to your head."

"Fine!" Uncle Fred shot back. "Then I'm getting out of here. Now!"

Deborah's mouth opened in a small O of surprise. "What's going on?" she whispered.

Before Leslie could answer, Uncle Fred exploded into the kitchen. Not even glancing at the girls, he rushed out the back door.

Trisha cast a horrified look at Leslie. Then she sucked in her breath and ran in the opposite direction, into the party.

Quickly, Leslie darted after her, bumping into people in all directions. Trisha was nowhere to be seen.

"Leslie!" Her grandmother called her over. "There's something I want to tell you."

Granny's voice brimmed with emotion, and for the moment, Trisha slipped from Leslie's mind.

Leslie looked at her grandmother curiously. Granny was usually so calm and cool. Right now she sounded agitated. Whatever she wanted to tell her must be important. The people and the party melted away. Leslie concentrated on her grandmother.

Kneeling by her grandmother's side, Leslie clasped her hand.

"Leslie," the old woman continued, "I am eighty years old. My time is almost here. I am approaching the end."

Leslie jerked up her head, startled. "No, Granny. Please don't talk that way."

"Shh, my sweet child. There is nothing to be afraid of. I've led a long, full life. And when I look at you, I see the future. My future. I feel immortal." She held up her hand. The skin glowed with a translucent shimmer, and the hand seemed paper thin. It hit Leslie that her grandmother was well and truly old. Granny Barrows shifted her hand, and her emerald sparkled in the dim light.

"The emerald is our birthstone," she told Leslie quietly. "This ring and all my jewelry will be yours someday."

"Enough secrets!" A loud, accented voice cut through the air. The rest of the room flooded back to Leslie. She sat back on her heels, remembering the party.

"Enough!" the voice repeated. Leslie stiffened. Mrs. Krashmer, Granny's best friend, hovered over them, her round dark eyes flashing.

Granny and Mrs. Krashmer had grown up together in Eastern Europe, and after all the years and all the changes, they were still inseparable. Leslie couldn't understand why. The two women couldn't be more different. Mrs. Krashmer acted as if she'd never set foot on American soil, wearing shapeless black clothes and dark scarves. She stuck close to the people she'd known in her old village and lived her old-world ways.

Leslie pulled back from Mrs. Krashmer. The old woman had a funny smell. Dark hairs sprouted from a mole on her face. And when she smiled at Leslie, her swollen red gums glistened.

"It is time for your birthday present, Leslie," Mrs. Krashmer said in her hoarse, commanding voice. "Come with me."

Leslie looked questioningly at her grandmother. Mrs. Krashmer had never given her anything before. And the idea of opening her gift filled Leslie with an odd feeling of dread. But when her grandmother nodded at her to follow, Leslie allowed herself to be led away.

In the kitchen, Trisha was sitting at the table, waiting. Deborah was gone. "She got you, too?" Trisha whispered.

Leslie nodded as she sat down. She wanted to ask Trisha if she was okay. But Mrs. Krashmer stood over the girls, waiting to get their attention. She leaned close to Leslie. Her breath smelled of garlic. "For your gifts," she hissed, "I will tell your fortunes."

She pushed two cups of tea toward Leslie and Trisha. "Drink, drink," she urged. "When you are done, you will hear your futures."

Fortunes? Futures? That was a little much, just a little too dramatic — even for Mrs. Krashmer, Leslie thought. True, the old woman did have a strange reputation. A reputation for having a sixth sense, a second sight.

Her grandmother had told Leslie many times about Mrs. Krashmer predicting births and deaths, sickness, even the weather. And Leslie did half believe in that sort of stuff — superstitions, fate, or whatever you called it — at least when it concerned other people. She watched all the made-for-TV movies — movies where people are warned about their future but are powerless to change it. But for her, in her life, doom and gloom and fortune-telling seemed way out of place.

"Drink!" Mrs. Krashmer urged again.

Leslie gulped down the hot liquid, burning the roof of her mouth. The tea left a sharp, bitter aftertaste. Leslie curled her tongue, wrinkling her nose in displeasure. Then she slid the cup over, eager to be rid of it.

Trisha drank more slowly, taking her time. "Da da da da — dum," she hummed under her breath, imitating music from a scary movie.

Outside, the skies opened up and rain lashed the windows. A crack of lightning jolted Trisha, and the last of the tea sloshed into her saucer.

Mrs. Krashmer reached for both cups, then gazed at the tea leaves intently. Another bolt of lightning illuminated Mrs. Krashmer's face. Her large dark eyes opened wide. Suddenly, she seemed frightened.

Leslie gripped the table. Every terrifying movie plot she'd ever seen roared back to mind.

"There will be trouble," Mrs. Krashmer said in her heavy accent. "Grave trouble for you both before your sixteenth birthdays."

Leslie's heart pounded louder than the thunder. This was no movie of the week. This was her life. Her safe, normal life. "What?" she said in a strangled voice. "What do you — "

But she didn't get any further. Shouts and cries sounded from the living room.

Leslie's mother rushed into the kitchen, her face a deathly shade of white. "Call an ambulance," she cried.

Granny Barrows had collapsed.

PART TWO

April 1996

Chapter 2

"Leslie! Breakfast!" Mrs. Barrows called from the kitchen. Upstairs in her room, Leslie ran a brush through her tangled red hair. "I'll be right there," she shouted back.

It was Friday morning, and as usual, Leslie was running late for school. No matter how hard she tried, it seemed, she just couldn't make herself be on time. "Chronic lateness," her father often joked, "is becoming a way of life for you. Good thing it's your only fault."

Leslie's parents thought she was just about perfect. Perfect manners. Perfect study habits. A perfect sense of responsibility. But what good did those things do? Leslie knew, in fact, those perfect little traits were really glaring faults. She was way too responsible. Too well-mannered. In other words, boring.

Last year, during her first year of high school, the year she was supposed to break free, experiment, rebel a little, what did she do? She hung out with her boyfriend Steve and her best friend Deborah, studying at the library, going to lectures at the local college, and renting old movies. The three spent so much time together, doing the kinds of things her parents approved of, she'd barely been alone with Steve. That's how good she was.

But maybe all that would change, now that she'd broken up with serious-minded Steve. Now that she was with Rick.

Leslie glanced at her alarm clock. Seven-fifteen. Not bad, considering she'd just gotten out of bed fifteen minutes ago. Already she was showered and dressed, and putting the final touches on her makeup.

Leslie leaned closer to the mirror on her dresser, mascara wand in hand. "What do you you think, Granny?" she asked the picture taped to the corner of the mirror. "Am I laying it on a bit thick?"

Grinning at her grandmother's photo, Leslie decided, no. She wasn't wearing too much makeup. Just enough. Leave it to Granny and her penetrating stare to get the message across in a picture, since she couldn't do it in person.

Granny had died right after her eightieth birthday party. Leslie wasn't sure exactly what happened. All she knew was, her grandmother had a stroke and never completely recovered.

Three years had passed. It seemed like a long time; so much had happened, so much had changed. But Leslie still missed her grandmother, missed her strong forceful presence. Keeping her picture nearby helped. Leslie could almost feel her grandmother's love just looking at it.

In the photo, Granny Barrows was fifteen — about to turn sixteen — the same age as Leslie. Peering at the picture, Leslie wound her long, thick hair into a bun — the same 1920s style Granny wore — and smiled again. The two looked so alike, they could pass for twins.

Leslie's gaze shifted to the other picture in the mirror, her new boyfriend, Rick. Leslie couldn't really remember her grandfather. He died when she was young. But Leslie's grandmother had married him when she was about Leslie's age. And judging from old photo albums, she thought Rick looked, maybe, a bit like him, too.

For a moment Leslie daydreamed she was walking down the aisle, with blond, handsome Rick waiting for her at the altar.

"Leslie!" her mother called again. "Are you coming down for breakfast or not?"

"Coming, Mom!" Leslie hurriedly gathered her books, her brush, and some pens and dumped them in her leather knapsack. Seven-thirty. Where had all that time gone?

Quickly Leslie skipped down the stairs and into the kitchen. A low, hard-edged voice stopped her short. "Hi, Les."

Trisha.

Leslie tugged on her right ear, trying to rein in her annoyance. Her cousin sat at the kitchen table, munching on toast as if it were the most natural thing in the world to have breakfast at Leslie's house — for the third straight day.

Trisha stared at her coolly, daring her to say something. Silently, Leslie slid into her chair. She poured a glass of orange juice, then scooped some scrambled eggs onto her plate. Trisha eyed her heaping dish. "Planning on working out later?" she asked pleasantly.

Leslie bit back a retort. She might not be a twig exactly, but she certainly wasn't fat.

Stay calm, Leslie told herself. Trisha's just getting on your case, same as she's been doing for the past three weeks.

Three weeks ago, almost to the day, Trisha's parents had finally separated. No one was surprised. They'd been arguing for years. Still, Leslie knew it must be rough for Trisha. Money was tight. Trisha's father had taken an apartment above a drugstore in a seedy part of town. Her mother had found a part-time job as a cashier. The last thing Trisha needed was another family blowout.

Pretending to sip her orange juice, Leslie looked over the glass at her cousin.

Trisha's hair was slightly duller than Leslie's, her hazel eyes lighter. Her nose was short, almost stubby — not the true Barrows nose. But still, the resemblance was there. Leslie had overheard relatives discussing them, saying Trisha looked like a washed-out version of Leslie. A pale imitation.

But now, with all her family problems, she'd taken on a strange, haunted look. It gives Trisha depth, Leslie thought. She's prettier than she's ever been before.

No wonder Steve asked her out.

Steve, along with Leslie's boyfriend Rick, was a junior at Medvale High — a year ahead of Leslie and Trisha. For most of Leslie's freshman year, she and Steve had dated. He was her first boyfriend, the first boy she really kissed.

But looking back, it seemed more like a friendship than anything else. Steve had always been so quiet and introspective, so into studying and science. He'd kept his feelings locked up tight. Romantic moments were few and far between. The longer they dated, the further apart they drifted.

Eventually, Leslie broke things off. But they'd wound up on good terms, and it wasn't awkward when Steve started dating Trisha.

"Is Steve picking you up here?" Leslie asked hopefully.

The cousins didn't have their licenses yet. They'd only recently finished driver's ed, and wouldn't take their road tests until their sixteenth birthdays. But it would be easy for Steve to swing by for Trisha on his way to school. His old Volkswagen probably knew the way by itself.

Trisha smiled sweetly. "No. I thought I'd catch a ride with you and Rick. That is, if you don't mind."

"Of course she doesn't mind," said Mrs. Barrows, coming into the kitchen.

Leslie sighed. Great. She'd have to share Rick with her cousin for the third morning in a row. It was bad enough being insulted over breakfast day afer day. . . .

Leslie's thoughts trailed off as a wave of guilt swept over her.

Leslie's mom insisted it was important for Trisha to feel welcome in their home. "Aunt May doesn't do anything but watch TV," she'd confided to Leslie. "She doesn't turn on the lights when it gets dark, and she's always forgetting to cook meals. It's so depressing over there. Trisha needs some stability."

"How's your mom?" Mrs. Barrows asked now, concerned.

Trisha lowered her head and stared at the table. "All right, I guess. She's hooked on those TV talk shows." She lifted her eyes to Leslie's. "Not the most endearing quality in a person. But at least *she* doesn't confuse it with reality."

Leslie's mother rattled some pots by the sink, oblivious to the barbed remark. But Leslie recognized the comment for what it was — a direct put-down of Deborah Shaw.

From her thirteenth birthday on, Leslie had grown closer and closer with Deborah. When Leslie needed someone to talk to about her grandmother's death, someone who had a little distance, who wasn't part of the family, she had turned to Deborah. Maybe it was because she'd been at the party that night. The two had long talks, starting with love. Then clothes and boys and movies.

Deborah had been the first person Leslie called when Steve asked her out. And she'd been the first person she cried to when they broke up.

But lately — after she started dating Rick,

Leslie realized — Deborah had turned away from her. She'd started watching those TV talk shows, quoting the hosts and panelists like old friends. Recently she'd been taping the morning and afternoon shows so she wouldn't miss a single one.

Deborah did take things to extremes, sure, but Trisha didn't have to get nasty.

Leslie swallowed hard. Trisha's going through a rough time, she repeated to herself. Be nice. Be nice. It was like a chant to focus in the right direction. The nice, cousinly direction.

"We need your opinion, Trisha," Leslie's mother said, sitting down to join the girls. "We're starting to plan Leslie's Sweet Sixteen. We want to go all out, do something really amazing."

She squeezed Leslie's hand excitedly. "Sharon's coming down from college for the weekend to brainstorm with us. Do you want to come over, too? Maybe you have some ideas?"

Leslie coughed, choking on a bite of toast.

"I'm sorry, Aunt Miriam," Trisha said smoothly. "Steve and I are going to be busy all weekend. But thanks for including me."

Strangely enough, Leslie felt a little disappointed. When Trisha was in a good mood, she could be a lot of fun. And when her sarcasm wasn't quite so biting, she could be pretty funny, too.

The cousins really did have an odd relationship. But something connected them — blood, age, who knows — and sometimes Leslie glimpsed what it would be like to be close. Then she wished they could be friends — real friends — all over again.

Outside, an engine roared, then died away. Leslie heard a car door slam. Then Rick poked his head in the kitchen doorway. Just as always, Leslie's heart skipped a beat when she saw him.

A year ago, she'd never have thought they'd be going out. Rick wasn't really her type. Tall, blond, and all-American with a square chin and rugged features, he was the surfer you saw in magazine ads. The guy voted "Most Popular," with a sunny, open personality.

Before Rick, Leslie had felt a pull toward dark, brooding guys. The intellectual with his nose stuck in a book, or a loner with a dark, mysterious side. More like Steve, Leslie knew — someone you could imagine had a secret.

Or maybe she just stayed away from the handsome, popular guys because she thought they wouldn't be interested in her. She wasn't outgoing or wildly funny. She was more on the quiet side. A nice, good girl, Leslie reminded herself.

But whatever the reason, Leslie was crazy about Rick. More than crazy, she'd already decided. She was really and finally in love.

"How are my three favorite women?" Rick bent to peck Leslie on the cheek, then grinned at Mrs. Barrows and Trisha.

Mrs. Barrows giggled, and even Trisha broke into a smile. All at once, everything seemed perfect to Leslie: a perfect new boy-friend. A perfect family. And a perfect Sweet Sixteen just around the corner.

Talking and laughing, she and Trisha grabbed their knapsacks. "Your chariot awaits," Rick said grandly, leading the way to his brand-new convertible. The sun shone brightly, and Leslie felt almost light-headed with happiness.

"Come on, you guys!" squealed a high, squeaky voice from the car. "We don't have all day."

Leslie's happiness shattered into little bits, like a bright shiny mirror crashing to the floor.

Rick's old girlfriend, Caroline, sat in the front seat.

Chapter 3

"I'm sorry, Les," Rick whispered, his mouth close to her ear. "I couldn't get out of taking Caroline. You know how it is."

Leslie nodded grimly, sliding into the back-seat next to Trisha. She knew how Rick *thought* it was.

"Caroline's so sensitive, so vulnerable," he'd said time and time again. "I really hurt her when I broke up with her. Doing these little favors is the least I can do."

Then he'd grab Leslie's hand or stare deeply into her eyes. And no matter what Leslie had been about to say, no matter how she'd been about to protest, she'd melt and nod under-standingly.

"After all," Rick would usually add, "Caroline needs me. She's gotten so dependent on me. And here I am, going out with you, while she's all alone, miserable and mixed-up."

Leslie thought Caroline was anything but mixed-up. The girl knew exactly what she wanted, and Leslie had a feeling she'd go after it with a vengeance. As for being miserable, right now Caroline looked absolutely triumphant. Smiling broadly, she tossed her long blond hair over the car seat, so a strand blew in Leslie's face.

"Have you started that paper yet for Mr. Corr?" she asked Leslie. She didn't bother to turn around, so Leslie had to answer to the back of her head.

"Uh-uh," Leslie started to say.

"I haven't," Caroline broke in. Then she leaned close to Rick as he started the car. "But then again, Ricky's promised to help me, so I'm sure I won't have any problems. You probably don't know this, Leslie, since you don't know Rick very well, but he had Mr. Corr for history last year."

Trisha dug her elbow into Leslie's side, rolling her eyes. "You don't know Ricky very well," she whispered squeakily, imitating Caroline. "But he has to do all my work. You see, my shoe size is higher than my IQ." She batted her eyelashes, and Leslie stifled a laugh. She smiled warmly at her cousin.

There was that glimpse again, that glimmer of friendship.

For the rest of the drive, Caroline chattered on while Leslie stared out the window.

Why couldn't that perfect feeling she had in the kitchen last? Why couldn't she hold on to it a little while longer?

At last, Rick pulled up to a spot in Medvale High's busy parking lot.

"Good morning, Trisha." Steve lounged against his Volkswagen, then came over as everyone tumbled out of Rick's car. "I've been wondering when you'd get here."

Steve kept talking to Trisha, but he was looking straight at Leslie. "You're late again, Trisha, and I guess I know who to blame. Some things never change."

Steve had a sharp, thin nose, serious black eyes, and an even more serious expression.

What's gotten into him? Leslie wondered. I didn't make Trisha that late. But she didn't say anything. She just smiled as Steve and Trisha walked quickly away. Steve didn't care much for Rick, and he always hurried off as if he had an important exam he couldn't miss.

A few parking spots over, Deborah scrambled out of her car. Instantly spotting Leslie, she bounded over like a big shaggy dog. Her short brown hair bounced wildly with every step, and her loose-fitting cotton shirt flapped behind her. Deborah almost always wore men's button-down shirts, insisting to Leslie that they hid her flab.

"Leslie!" she shouted, almost hugging her friend with joy. "Today's the first day I drove to school." She eyed Rick's shiny black convertible. "Of course, I'm driving my parents' old station wagon. But come look! I just made a truly perfect park!"

She pulled Leslie away from Rick, gloating with every step. A few months older than Leslie, she'd just gotten her driver's license.

"Nice park," Leslie said absentmindedly, craning her neck to find Rick in the crowd. People were spilling out of the lot into the schoolyard. There were still a few minutes before school started. If she could get Rick alone for just a second, she'd start the school day off right. Well, maybe not right. But better, at least.

Leslie hated to admit it, but her superstitious streak had gotten worse over the past few years. If she broke a nail the same day she had a test, she felt certain she'd fail. If she missed a bus, she was certain Rick wouldn't call that night.

And if she didn't talk to Rick right now, she'd have a totally miserable day.

"Do you see Rick?" she asked Deborah, trying to keep the edge out of her voice.

"He's over there," Deborah answered grudgingly, "with the cast from *Snob Central*."

Snob Central! Leslie hadn't thought about that for weeks.

Snob Central was the fake TV show Deborah had concocted, starring the most popular kids in school in embarrassing situations. Leslie had gone along with it at first, because it was kind of fun. Even B.R. — Before Rick — she couldn't resist casting Caroline in a *Titanic* episode, in which, too busy blow-drying her long blond hair, she'd missed the last lifeboat.

But then Deborah focused on Rick. She had him in almost every scene — dropping the football in the final minutes of the championship game, splitting his jeans in the middle of the hall. Leslie drew back. She couldn't, just couldn't, lump Rick in with the rest of them. And maybe he somehow read her mind, because right afterward, he started acting interested. He'd stop by her lunch table in the cafeteria, stare at her in the library. Then one night he called her up and asked her out.

That's when Leslie asked Deborah to drop him from their little scenarios. A week or so later, much to Deborah's annoyance, she abandoned the whole *Snob Central* idea.

"How can I keep it up, when I'm hanging

out with these people?" she'd told Deborah. "I'm beginning to really like them. And you know we only started the whole thing out of jealousy anyway."

Deborah had snorted, turning away.

"Come on, Deborah," Leslie said now, trying to nudge her friend toward the group. "Why don't you try being nice to them? You'd be surprised how nice they are back."

"All those cheerleaders and jocks nice? To me? I don't think so."

"Oh, wait a minute," Deborah went on, digging her heels into the ground. "That reminds me of something. An idea for a talk show. I saw a couple of interesting ones yesterday that got me thinking. You have to hear about them."

Leslie caught sight of Rick in the middle of a group of pretty juniors, laughing and horsing around. If they could just edge a little closer . . .

"One was called Sour Sixteen," Deborah explained, moving along with Leslie and not even realizing it. "It was all about teenage girls" — she put on a loud, announcer-type voice — "who are anything but sweet."

Several of the girls turned their heads to stare at Deborah. Leslie wished they'd stayed where they were.

"And then I flipped the channel," Deborah continued, "and another show had all these strange women on. Fortune-tellers, you know, people with a sixth sense. And it all reminded me of Mrs. Krashmer and her weird prediction about your sixteenth birthday."

"Mrs. Krashmer?" Leslie said blankly.

The prediction had frightened her for months afterward, maybe even sparked her superstitious streak. She'd deliberately buried the spooky old woman deep in her memory. So now it took a moment to register — especially when she had one eye on Rick, and the other on Deborah, trying to send her friend a silent message: Hush up! Too many people are looking at us!

Donna, one of the prettiest girls in the crowd and Caroline's best friend, peeled herself away from the others. Rick had already disappeared. Probably carrying Caroline's books, Leslie thought dejectedly. Too bad everyone else couldn't disappear, too.

"Someone told your fortune?" Donna asked Leslie, dragging over a bunch of people. "What happened?"

"Nothing happened," Leslie protested. "It was just some crazy old woman trying to scare Trisha and me."

"Trisha too?" Donna rubbed her manicured

hands together. "Tell us more!"

A crowd of people — jocks, cheerleaders, and assorted *Snob Central* cast members — surrounded Deborah. A gleam of triumph seemed to come into her eyes. A look that said, these people want to talk to me. To me, plain old Deborah Shaw.

"Well," Deborah began uncertainly.

"Come on, Deb," Donna prodded in a friendly way. "Is there something in Leslie's past we should know about?"

"It's no big deal," Deborah finally said. "It's just this old woman — a friend of Leslie's grandmother — predicted trouble for Leslie and Trisha before their sixteenth birthdays." She shrugged. "That's all."

"That's all?" Donna's eyes lit up, as if she had hit the gossip jackpot. "Our Ricky is dating a woman who's doomed!"

Leslie was saved from replying. The school bell rang. She walked toward the building, her feet dragging heavily. Rick, of course, was nowhere in sight. And Leslie knew the day would only get worse.

Chapter 4

Leslie stole glance after glance at her wristwatch. But each time she looked, the hands were in the same exact spot. It was the last class of the day, and Leslie couldn't wait for it to end.

All morning and afternoon, she'd roamed the halls between classes searching for Rick. It had become a mission, tracking him down and speaking to him so she'd be able to relax for the rest of the day. But she hadn't had any luck. She hadn't seen him once.

But finally, thankfully, the school day was winding down. Leslie sat at her desk counting down the minutes, her head buried in her history book.

Whenever Mr. Corr grew tired of teaching, he'd tell them to read a chapter or two at their desks. It was a silly practice, one that would get him in trouble if any of the students reported it.

But today, Leslie was glad to be in Mr. Corr's class. She'd been right about the day getting worse. For the tenth time that afternoon, Leslie relived that ridiculous scene before school.

Why did Deb speak so loudly? she wondered again. Why did Donna have to herd everyone over? Why did they all make such a big deal about that silly prediction?

Leslie could tell they thought she was a joke. A nutcase. All her new friends, turning away, laughing at her. And then, on top of everything, she had to reassure Deborah, tell her she didn't care. That she wasn't angry or even embarrassed.

Embarrassed? Leslie felt a slow flush spread over her face just thinking about it. Quickly, she skipped to annoyance number two: that business in the car, with Caroline swooning all over Rick.

Caroline. There she sat, one seat down, one across from Leslie, her perfect blond head bent over her notebook. Perfectly pretty Caroline, cheerleader, teacher's pet. So sweet, everyone said. But people had short memories. It seemed only Leslie remembered an incident from junior high. A time when Caroline was crazy about a boy named Tommy Terroni.

For weeks Caroline had followed him around like a little lost puppy. She dogged his every step, mooning over him like some crazed, adoring fan. Eventually, his family moved away. Caroline moved on to other boyfriends, and soon everyone forgot her obsession.

But what would have happened if Tommy had stayed in Medvale and dated someone else? How would Caroline have reacted?

Leslie slid her eyes over to Caroline. She was scribbling furiously in her notebook.

Then she tore out a page, folded it up, and passed it to Leslie. Leslie knew what it was without even looking at the name on the front: a note for Donna, who sat to her right.

Donna reached out her hand and Leslie thrust the note toward her. But Mr. Corr raised his head at that exact moment, and Donna let the paper drop. It lay on the floor, slowly unfolding.

It wasn't a note. Not really. It was just a big heart with two names scrawled in the middle: "Caroline and Rick," with a great big "4-ever" after them, the kind of silly heart you drew in grade school with an arrow piercing through the center.

* * *

After class, Leslie stood at her locker, willing herself not to think about Caroline's warped obsession with Rick. She shows real artistic promise, Leslie thought, trying to laugh. Art must be the one class she doesn't need Rick's help in.

Then she spotted the small note taped under her lock.

"Ugh," Leslie groaned. "Another prized piece by Caroline?"

She ripped the square of paper open, then grinned. It was from Rick.

Leslie kept smiling as she read how he missed her terribly and felt absolutely awful about this morning. Could he make it up to her? He'd take her to the finest establishment in town: Tony's, the neighborhood pizza place.

Feeling her spirits rise, Leslie held the note close. There it was, the vaguest scent of Black Magic, Rick's favorite cologne. Leslie shut her eyes, sniffing happily. Lost in thought, she remembered the late-night embraces they shared, Rick's soft-as-a-butterfly kisses.

Slowly Leslie opened her eyes. She had the feeling someone was watching her.

Steve.

A few feet away, Steve locked eyes with her. He was talking to Trisha, but his gaze traveled over her shoulder to linger on Leslie.

To stare at her, really, a strange expression on his face. Fierce, almost possessive. A look she'd seen from time to time when they were together, when she'd talk to another guy or change their plans.

Leslie hoisted her books in her arms and took off.

"Hey! What's your hurry?" Rick stepped in front of her and looped his arm around her shoulder.

Leslie laughed. That feeling she'd had early in the morning, the feeling that all was right with the world, rushed back. Caroline and that heart? It didn't mean a thing. "I was hurrying to meet you at Tony's."

Rick put on a fake displeased expression. "Don't you know by now that when you have a date with Richard Lewis Conlon, you get the red-carpet treatment all the way? My girlfriend never walks. She rides!"

Rick loped easily to his black convertible idling by the curb. He pulled open the passenger door, bowing ceremoniously to Leslie. "Madame," he said in a chauffeur-type voice. "Your car is here."

Giggling, Leslie pretended to lift her skirt to slide inside. Rick ran around to the driver's side, folded his tall body into the seat, and then gunned the engine.

"You know, Rick," Leslie said as he turned the corner, "I have my learner's permit now. It would be great if you'd let me drive once in a while, to practice."

"Why would you want to drive," Rick teased, "when I'm here to chauffeur you around? I tell you, Les, life doesn't get much better than this."

He switched on the radio and fiddled with the dials until he came to Leslie's favorite station.

Rick reached over to stroke her hair. "Anything special you want to listen to?" he asked. "We don't have to keep the radio on. I've got lots of CDs in the glove compartment."

A picture flashed in Leslie's mind: the heart with "Caroline and Rick" inscribed in the center, beating, pulsing like a real one. Alive and healthy.

Should she mention the heart to Rick?

Leslie rifled through the CDs while she considered her question. No, she decided. She didn't have the heart to make Rick feel bad about Caroline again. She'd keep it to herself for now.

"Whatever you want to listen to is fine," she said out loud, handing Rich the CDs when he stopped at a light.

At Tony's, Rick insisted on playing waiter,

serving her pizza, and even paying for it. Leslie leaned back against his arm, feeling safe and secure.

Rick really was the perfect boyfriend. Always sweet. Always cheerful. She would tell him about Caroline when the time was right . . . he'd definitely understand. But for now, Leslie brushed Caroline and her nasty ways into the far corner of her mind.

"You're way too good to me," she whispered to Rick. "What would I do without you?"

Chapter 5

Leslie spent Friday night with her family. As promised, Sharon had come down from college, and they'd all sat around the kitchen table, plotting every step of Leslie's Sweet Sixteen. They'd stayed up past midnight, thinking up ideas, ironing out difficulties. Already, Leslie felt like the center of attention.

The whole thing had been fun but exhausting, and Leslie wanted to sleep in on Saturday morning. Instead, she woke up with a start when the telephone rang at 7:30.

Maybe it's Rick, she thought, stretching lazily for the receiver. Calling to say he missed me last night and wants to spend every waking moment with me today. "Hello," she mumbled into the phone, still half asleep.

"Leslie!" Deborah's voice boomed urgently through the wire. Leslie sat up with a jerk.

"Deborah! Is something wrong?"

"No. Why would you think something's wrong?"

Leslie leaned back against her pillow. "Well, maybe because you're calling at the crack of dawn."

"Oh. Well, I just wanted to catch you. I know you're probably going out with Rick tonight — just like you've been doing every Saturday night." Deborah's voice rose, and Leslie tensed. Would she want to come along? Leslie didn't feel ready for that quite yet.

"Anyway," Deborah continued, "I thought we could get together this afternoon. I just saw a Sally Jessy Raphael on party planning, and I taped it for you. You should check it out for your Sweet Sixteen."

"I wish I could," Leslie said, choosing each word carefully, "but you know Sharon's home to help with my Sweet Sixteen, and she's taking me shopping for a dress, and then we're going to look at restaurants and stuff like that with my parents."

Leslie had kept her voice level, but now it grew loud with excitement. She hopped out of bed, twisting the phone line around her finger. "We stayed up late last night, and everything's practically all worked out. I wouldn't really need the Sally Jessy tape anyway."

"Oh, really?" Deborah sounded a little put out.

"I have to tell you the plans," Leslie continued excitedly. "The party's going to be an all-day celebration. We're renting out an entire skating rink for the afternoon. Then in the evening we'll go to a really nice restaurant. You know, where we'll have to get dressed up? Isn't that great?"

Deborah was silent on the other end. Plopping down on her bed, Leslie felt her spirits drop. Why couldn't everyone be happy at the same time? Why did Deborah feel so lousy, when she was feeling so great?

Finally Deborah spoke, her voice less than enthusiastic. "It really does sound wonderful, Les. How about tomorrow? Could we grab a bite to eat on Sunday?"

"Sure," Leslie began. "We'll — "

And then she stopped. She'd just remembered her history paper, due on Monday. She'd barely started it, and she'd have to spend all day Sunday working on it.

"I'm sorry, Deb. It's just not possible."

Leslie heard Deborah's voice catch. "Oh, please don't be upset," Leslie cried quickly. "It's just that I have so much to do!"

Deborah got hold of herself and said, "I understand, Leslie. At least I'm trying to. But when you were going out with Steve, I could always hang out with you guys. He always made me feel welcome. In fact, Les, there's something I have to tell you." Deborah's voice warmed. "Steve's always been so great to me. Going out of his way to be nice and stuff. I think — "

"Yes, yes," Leslie interrupted, suddenly impatient with the conversation. She had a million things to do, and since Deborah had woken her up, she might as well get a jump on them. "You think Steve's a good friend, too.

"And you know, you can hang out with Rick and me soon," she promised, just as suddenly feeling guilty. "But right now our relationship is still too new for that sort of thing. And everything is a little weird because of Caroline."

"Sure, sure," Deborah said. But she sounded more angry than soothed. "And now that I think of it, I've got lots to do without you. I've got a whole bunch of talk shows on tape I have to watch."

Deborah slammed the phone down, and Leslie was left listening to a dial tone.

Leslie gently hung up. She toyed with the idea of dropping by to see Deborah, but decided against it. When Deb gets like this, she reasoned, the best thing to do is leave her alone. Let her simmer down, then she'd come around.

She always had before.

The line for the movies snaked around the block. Once again it had taken Leslie longer than she intended to get ready. And now, standing at the back of the line, it seemed she and Rick would be stuck in a back corner of the theater, craning their necks to see the screen.

"*Kiss of Darkness* has been playing for weeks now," Rick said, his arm around Leslie. "I wasn't expecting this big a crowd. Otherwise I would have rushed you more."

Leslie smiled up at him. "Well, it is Saturday night. Maybe people are seeing it again."

"It's the second time I'm seeing it," Donna piped up behind them.

At the sound of Donna's voice, Leslie winced. She had been surprised to find Donna and her boyfriend, Brian, waiting in the backseat of Rick's convertible when he'd picked her up.

"I hope you don't mind," Rick had whispered. "But they called, wanting to get together, and I couldn't say no."

Brian, blond like Rick, had a thick neck and a big football-player build. He was Rick's best friend. But Leslie didn't feel very comfortable with him yet. He reminded her of the husbands in those creepy made-for-TV movies about fortunes and predictions — the dense, thick-headed characters who never believed their wives until it was too late.

Brian chuckled. "Yeah, there's nothing like taking a date to a vampire movie. Come, show me your neck. I want my kiss good night. Now!" Brian spoke with an accent right from the film.

Everyone laughed uproariously, as if it were the funniest thing they'd ever heard. Leslie tried to smile and look amused. But the accent smacked of Eastern Europe, reminding Leslie of her grandmother . . . of Mrs. Krashmer . . . and the laugh choked in her throat.

"Hey! Isn't that Gwen and Barry up front?" Brian peered over the line of people's heads. "Yup! It is. Let's go join them. We'll get better seats."

Leslie's heart sank. She didn't feel right jumping ahead of everyone on line, but already the other three were moving forward. Rick grabbed her hand, and she let him pull her along. When they reached Gwen and Barry,

Leslie realized a whole crew of their friends were there, too. It had turned into a big group outing.

Great, Leslie thought. This just gets better and better. But, she thought thankfully, Caroline hadn't come. And, Leslie realized just as thankfully, no one had mentioned that scene in school the other day, where everyone had been so interested in Mrs. Krashmer and the prediction. Smiling grimly, Leslie resolved to enjoy herself, to have fun.

That's why she was going out with Rick, wasn't it?

For a moment, Leslie tried to picture Deborah with this whole gang of laughing, joking people. Maybe next time she'd bring her. It might not be so bad. If you didn't concentrate too hard on their jokes, they could even be kind of funny.

The line moved along with everyone kidding around, and Leslie relaxed. When Brian made another vampire joke about necking, Leslie laughed louder than anyone else. And when Donna complimented her on her lacy white blouse, Leslie felt like she was finally fitting in.

At the ticket window, Rick whipped out his wallet before Leslie could protest, and before she knew it, they were inside the lobby. Rick dashed off to buy popcorn and soda.

Donna stood next to Leslie, checking her makeup while Brian went to the candy counter. "So have you finished that paper for Corr?" she asked.

Leslie shook her head ruefully. "I'll work on it tomorrow. This weekend I've been so busy with Sweet Sixteen plans, I haven't had time for anything else."

She told Donna about the ice-skating party in the afternoon, Flamingo's Restaurant where she had made reservations for the evening, and the long velvet dress she bought at Fiona's.

"It sounds amazing," Donna said. "My Sweet Sixteen was a family dinner at Danny's Burgerama. Not the best of celebrations, but hey — we did get all-you-could-eat sundaes."

Donna grinned, and Leslie smiled back. Maybe she and Donna could even be friends.

Leslie hadn't given much thought to the guest list yet, but of course she'd have to invite Donna. And now that she was hanging out with all Rick's friends, maybe Gwen and the others, too.

"I'm going to invite everyone!" Leslie said impulsively. She waved her arms to include the rest of the group, and the girls came over to find out more.

"Hey, what's the big conference about?" Leslie turned to Rick as he lurched toward them. He was balancing a big tub of popcorn with one hand and two jumbo sodas in the other, and seemed to be having trouble.

"Here, let me help you." Leslie reached out to grab the sodas at the same time Rick stumbled forward. They collided. The big paper cups tilted wildly. Leslie, rushing to save them, hugged the cups close. Bright orange soda bubbled out.

"Oh!" Leslie gasped as the colorful liquid spilled down her new white blouse.

She righted the cups quickly. But it was too late. The damage was done. A sticky orange mess covered the whole front of her shirt.

For a moment, there was silence while Donna and Brian and the others looked surprised, and Leslie didn't move.

"Here!" cried Rick, springing into action. He hauled over a heap of napkins, then dabbed at her awkwardly. "You can hardly see a thing."

Leslie eyed the big orange stain doubtfully. Her favorite shirt was ruined — and now she'd have to walk around like the "before" picture in a laundry detergent ad for the rest of the evening.

"It's pretty hard to miss," she said.

Donna clapped her hand over her mouth in an exaggerated fashion. "Oh my gosh! The prediction about your sixteenth birthday. It's coming true!"

"Yeah, right," Leslie said, deciding to go along with the joke. "I wonder what will happen next? Maybe I'll drop a slice of pizza in my lap. Or a scoop of ice cream will roll off my ice-cream cone."

"Seriously, though" — Donna paused to wet a napkin at the water fountain, before wiping the stain more thoroughly — "doesn't that whole thing make you a little nervous?"

Leslie paused before she answered, wondering how she could play the fortune-telling down. Really, she wanted to forget the entire prediction. Because if she did think about it — really think about it — she'd be more than a little nervous.

But she couldn't tell anyone that, could she?

Finally Leslie began to speak. But before her "Of course I'm not nervous" even left her lips, Rick had pulled his light blue sweater over his head and was tugging it over Leslie's, muffling her words.

"There," he said, almost boastfully. "That takes care of the stain problem."

Leslie pulled her hair out of the sweater, grateful but at the same time annoyed. Rick had surprised her — and he hadn't even given her a chance to finish her sentence.

"Besides," Rick went on, answering Donna's question. "Why should Leslie be nervous?" Squeezing Leslie tight, he added, "She's got me to protect her."

Leslie felt uncomfortable — and it was more than the sticky blouse plastered to her skin, she realized. Rick was always doing little favors for her: chauffeuring her around, never letting her drive or pay for one little thing when they were together.

But I'm not helpless, Leslie told herself. I'm not like Caroline, who needs Rick's help to tie her shoes. I can take care of myself.

Still, it felt so good to have Rick's strong arms around her. To know he'd be there to protect her. His sweater smelled of Black Magic, and it hung almost to her knees. Everyone could tell she was wearing her boyfriend's sweater. A sweet warm feeling traveled right to her toes. So Leslie didn't protest . . . didn't say what she really felt. She just snuggled up closer.

And that's when she heard it.

A high-pitched giggle. A mocking laugh that sounded more like a shriek. No one else seemed to notice. They broke up into couples, and shuffled into the theater. But Leslie could have sworn she saw a flash of blond hair disappear around the corner. And only one person could have a laugh like that.

Caroline.

Chapter 6

Now how did this strange group get together? Leslie wondered.

It was Tuesday afternoon, a few days after her *Kiss of Darkness* date, and Leslie sat at the head of a long table in the high school cafeteria.

Her eyes wandered over the crowded table, noting who was there. Steve and Trisha. Deborah. Donna and Brian and Rick, of course, and some of their friends. What an odd collection.

Usually Rick's friends clustered around the prime picnic table, right in the middle of the grassy campus quadrangle. But the rain was coming down in cold steady sheets, so everyone had gathered indoors.

As for Steve, he generally ate his lunch in the library or an empty classroom, his head bent over a book. But after he'd gotten his sandwich from the lunch counter, he'd seen Leslie tossing her knapsack on a table, and quickly dragged Trisha over to join her.

He hadn't realized that Leslie was saving the table. That Rick and the others would be descending on them any minute. Steve — quiet, withdrawn Steve — had insisted to Trisha that Leslie shouldn't eat alone. And he spoke so intently, so seriously, Trisha had nodded, unable to disagree.

Then Deborah grabbed a seat just as Rick and his gang swooped down like a tornado.

Now Deborah sat sandwiched between Brian and another one of their buddies at the other end of the table. She looked miserable, picking nervously at her tuna sandwich, not daring to lift her head for more than a second.

Trisha and Steve sat on Leslie's right, Rick to her left. Trisha pointedly kept her back to Leslie, bowing her head toward Steve. "I told you," she whispered heatedly, "this wasn't a very good idea."

Donna, on the outskirts of the group, tilted her chair toward the aisle. Leslie was surprised to see Donna on the fringe. She liked to be smack dab in the center of things. But then Leslie realized Caroline was sitting at the next table, and Donna was drawing the two groups together.

Who cares if Caroline is hanging around? Leslie tried to reassure herself. Not me.

At the movie theater the other night, she'd decided to just ignore Caroline. She would live her own life, not worry about Rick's past. Not even if one old girlfriend was a gorgeous, slightly crazy blond intent on getting him back.

Noise filled the high-ceilinged cafeteria. Voices rang out, silverware clattered, the cash register buzzed. A paper airplane flew through the air, landing in Deborah's lap. All eyes turned to her.

"Hey!" Caroline squealed. "Maybe someone sent you a love letter special delivery. Open it up!"

Deborah flushed as she tossed the paper aside. "Not very likely," she muttered.

Leslie pantomimed a huge yawn. "I am so tired!" she exclaimed, wanting to draw attention away from her friend. "I stayed up last night finishing my history paper on Winston Churchill, how he led England during World War Two."

Trisha yawned even wider than Leslie. "Sounds thrilling."

Leslie gritted her teeth. She would not let Trisha get to her.

"Well, the subject was actually kind of interesting," she explained in a voice that matched Trisha's hard-edged tone. "Did you know that Churchill's mom was American? She grew up in Brooklyn."

"Amazing," Trisha said.

Leslie sighed. Why was she trying to impress people with a history paper, of all things?

"Besides," she went on, "every time I took a break, my mom and I worked on invitations for the Sweet Sixteen."

"Just wait until you see them!" Rick broke in. He put his arm around Leslie. "Show them, Les!"

Leslie hesitated. The handmade invitations were in the shape of little ice skates with actual laces and real pom-poms. She'd spent hours working on them. But she'd only brought them to school so she could drop them at the post office later. Passing them around would ruin the surprise — not to mention the invitations.

"Yes," Trisha drawled. "Let's see those *darling* invitations we've heard so much about."

Leslie shot her a look. But really, when it came right down to it, how could she resist showing them off?

Digging into her knapsack, she found Rick's invitation, and passed it to Trisha. Barely glancing at it, Trisha passed it to Steve. Steve held it carefully, examining it as if it were some kind of lab experiment.

"Let's sneak off for a kiss," Rick whispered suddenly, pulling Leslie away from the table. Leslie felt Steve's eyes shoot straight from the invitation to the back of her head.

But she couldn't resist sinking into Rick's broad chest. The next few minutes passed in a haze — sweet kisses, mumbled endearments, all in a dark shadowy corner of the cafeteria. She forgot about Deborah sitting awkwardly with the cast from *Snob Central*. She forgot about Steve's dark piercing eyes. Trisha's sharp tongue. Caroline's jealous streak.

She forgot everyone but Rick.

The bell sounded suddenly; lunch was over. Hastily rushing back to the table, Leslie shoved Rick's invitation back into her knapsack. Then she pulled the bag onto her shoulder with surprising ease. That morning it felt a little different, more cumbersome, but she didn't have time to wonder. She gave Rick a quick kiss good-bye, and hurried off to gym.

It wasn't until history, when Leslie reached into her knapsack for her paper, that she realized something was wrong.

No! Her mind raced as she groped, desperately fumbling around her books. They have to be here. They have to!

Frantic now, Leslie turned the knapsack over. Everything tumbled out, scattering onto the floor. Books. History paper. Wallet. Leslie knelt down, searching through the items.

No, no, no! She dug back into her knapsack. Maybe they were stuck inside. Caught inside a flap or something.

No again. The knapsack was empty.

The invitations were gone.

Chapter 7

Apologizing to Mr. Corr, Leslie raced back to the cafeteria. The invitations were probably lying on the floor somewhere, hidden under a chair. They had to be!

Leslie searched the entire cafeteria once, twice, then one more time. Finally she realized it was useless. There was nothing to do but go back to class.

Slowly, Leslie stumbled back to the room. Caroline smiled at her cheerfully as she sank into her seat. "Hey, Leslie, don't worry about it," Caroline whispered in a falsely concerned tone. "Sometimes things just disappear. Just the other week it seems I had a boyfriend. And then — poof! — he was gone."

Leslie tensed, waiting for the next sentence.

"But I guarantee you," Caroline hissed, "I'm

going to find him again real soon."

Leslie let the remark roll off her, too upset to pay attention to half-crazy comments — and too busy as well. As soon as class ended, she ran out to buy ordinary, run-of-the-mill invitations from the local card shop. Then she quickly filled them in and sent them out.

It was not terribly difficult work, but it was disappointing and time-consuming. She'd planned on spending the afternoon taking care of little errands, and the invitations threw her all off schedule. A few days later, she still hadn't caught up, and by Friday afternoon, she was really running late.

Gazing at the big digital clock over her head, Leslie tapped her toe impatiently. Five twenty-seven. She was supposed to meet Trisha right here, under the giant clock in Medvale Mall, at five o'clock. Where was she? True, Leslie'd just gotten there herself. But Leslie was always late, and Trisha was always punctual.

To be honest, Leslie wasn't crazy about meeting Trisha at all. Not after the way she'd acted at lunch the other day, making snide comments about the invitations and her history paper.

Leslie knew Trisha wasn't keen on this little

get-together either. It was their mothers' doing — once again throwing the girls together, hoping they'd grow to be more than cousins.

"You need a new skating outfit for the party," Leslie's mother had said. "And so does Trisha. Why don't the two of you go together?"

"But Mom," Leslie had started to say.

"Let me rephrase that. The two of you *are* going together."

So now, Leslie was waiting for Trisha so they could do something neither of them wanted to do. Leslie glanced up at the clock. Five thirty-seven. Was Trisha deliberately keeping her waiting? Leslie wouldn't put it past her.

"Hi, Les." Leslie jumped at the sound of Trisha's voice behind her. "Hope you haven't been waiting long."

Leslie whirled around to peer at her curiously. "Oh!" she gasped. Her eyes widened in surprise. "What happened to you?"

Trisha wore the same jeans and green-striped sweater Leslie had seen dozens of times. But from the neck up she looked totally different, like some stone-age version of Trisha — a cave woman who'd chopped off all her hair with a dull ax.

"What happened to your hair?"

Trisha gave a strangled laugh. "Do you like it? It's the latest rage. I saw it in a fashion magazine and decided it was me."

Trisha's face crumpled suddenly, the pretense disappearing. Automatically, Leslie went to put her arm around her, to comfort her. Then she stopped. This was Trisha. Trisha who liked to keep her distance.

"Really," Leslie said softly. "Tell me what happened."

Hunching her shoulders, Trisha walked slowly to a nearby bench. She sat down, keeping her face hidden. "I just got out of Hair 'N Now."

"The haircutting place at the other end of the mall?"

Trisha nodded. "That's why I'm late. The hairdresser tried to fix this miserable cut. But the more she tried, the shorter it got and the worse it looked."

Gazing at the close-cropped hair, clumps sticking in different directions, Leslie settled next to her cousin. "But I've gone there." Unconsciously, Leslie touched her own soft hair. "All the stylists are really good. How could this have happened?"

Trisha drew in her breath. "Well, it wasn't really the stylist's fault." Her voice wavered.

"I'm sorry. I'm not telling this very well."

"That's all right. Just go ahead."

"You see," Trisha continued more steadily, "Deborah called me after school today. She wanted me to go with her for a haircut."

Leslie shook her head, confused. "Deborah called *you*? Since when do you two hang out together?"

"We don't. Not really. But she wanted to talk." Trisha ducked her head, almost shyly. "I think she misses you. Anyway, she sounded so unhappy, I couldn't say no."

Trisha smiled, once again cool and ironic. "I guess I'm getting to be a softie in my old age. Anyway, I figured I had to meet you here anyway, and Deborah offered to pick me up and drive me. Then, somehow, she convinced me I needed a haircut, too.

"Well, I'm already at the place. And I like the job the hairstylist did on Deborah. So I climb into the chair. And the next thing I know, Deborah is jumping all around like her pants are on fire, shouting there's a huge bug crawling up her sleeve. The stylist was so surprised, she cut a huge chunk of hair right out of my head."

Trisha sighed. "And you know the rest." She turned to Leslie, her eyes flooded with tears. "I can't believe my hair's so messed up!

I could have killed Deborah! But then she felt so bad, she started to cry. . . ."

"But where's Deborah now? Why didn't she come with you?"

"She just wanted to go home." Trisha grinned. "And I'm the one who should be hiding under the covers with this nightmare of a haircut."

Trisha reached out and touched Leslie's hand. "But Leslie, please don't say anything to Deborah about all this. It'll make her feel even worse."

Leslie leaned back, considering. Had this business somehow made Trisha softer, more human? It could just be the haircut, framing her face differently, giving her a younger, more vulnerable look. But maybe it was more. Maybe she was really turning to Leslie for comfort. Maybe she realized how important family could be.

Whatever the reason, this other side of Trisha — one Leslie had suspected all along — was a definite improvement.

"Of course I won't say anything to Deb," she responded. "Or anyone else. But how about we change our shopping schedule?"

Getting up, Leslie pulled Trisha to her feet. "First stop, the hat store!"

* * *

Leslie found a green baseball cap to match Trisha's sweater. Laughing, she set it on her cousin's head, and a few minutes later the girls were strolling through the mall, stopping now and then to window-shop.

Blades, the skating store, had everything in its window from in-line gear to hockey sticks to the latest fashions. "You know," Leslie said as they paused in front, "we've both had bad luck, Trisha. I lost my invitations. And now you got this crazy haircut."

Maybe, Leslie didn't say out loud, we have more in common than we thought.

Trisha pulled the cap down over her forehead, checking her reflection in the window. "As usual, you got the better end of the deal. Those new invitations you sent out were just fine, but I bet this haircut will take forever to grow out."

Trisha moaned, trying to fluff out the cut with her fingertips. "And my bad luck continues. Just the other day I lost my rose-petal earrings."

"The silver ones?"

"Uh-huh. I loved those earrings. They were kind of my good-luck charm — I wore them when I aced that English mid-term. And I was wearing them the first time Steve asked me out."

Immediately, Leslie felt another jolt of recognition. Good-luck earrings. Could Trisha be superstitious, too? This was a side to her cousin she'd never seen. Something she could relate to.

"Did you check everywhere?" Leslie asked, eager to be helpful. Trisha stepped inside the store and Leslie followed, listening closely to the answer.

"Everywhere! My house, your house, Steve's car, school. But they're gone. Gone, Gone, gone." Trisha shook her head. "It's like they disappeared."

"Just like my invitations," Leslie said grimly.

"Maybe losing things runs in our family." Trisha shrugged. "Who knows?" she added jokingly. "Maybe it's part of old Mrs. Krashmer's prediction."

Leslie grinned, then turned her attention to shopping. She tried on a half dozen different outfits, finally settling on a pretty light-blue set: a short twirly skirt with a soft fuzzy sweater to match.

"What about you?" she asked Trisha, going over to join her cousin at the sale rack.

Trisha flipped through the ragged-looking outfits. The colors were faded on some, the sleeves unravelling on others. Trisha checked a tag on one that seemed to be in reasonably good shape. "A twelve!" she muttered. "And that's the closest one to my size, too."

"You didn't like any on the regular racks?" Leslie said a little hesitantly. She didn't want to come right out and ask, "Is this all you can afford?"

"Forget it." Trisha said. She walked over to the cashier and waited for Leslie. "I'm going to hold off buying anything for a while. I want to talk to my mom. See if my dad came through with a check yet."

Trisha spoke offhandedly, almost as if she didn't care about the money, or not getting an outfit. Leslie got the feeling she had other things on her mind. But it was still an awkward situation, buying this expensive outfit for a spare-no-expense party.

Feeling a little embarrassed, Leslie rummaged through her wallet searching for her parents' credit card. She almost offered to put Trisha's outfit on the card, too. But she thought that would only make it worse.

Hurry, she pleaded silently to the slow-moving cashier. Let's get this over with.

Finally, the outfit bagged and stowed out of sight in her knapsack, Leslie led Trisha out of the store. "Let's see," she said, checking her list of things to do. "I should go to that restaurant we made reservations at, Flamingo's, to go over the menu. Do you want to come?"

Trisha nodded absentmindedly. "You know," she said thoughtfully, "money's been tight since my parents split. But I don't even really care. The whole thing's gotten me thinking about stuff that's a lot more important."

Leslie sighed, relieved. Maybe she should have offered to pay for Trisha's outfit after all.

She was just about to bring it up when Trisha dropped a bombshell. "I'm thinking about breaking up with Steve."

Leslie stopped walking. "What? What does that have to do with anything? I thought things were going so well!"

"Well, things are okay. But that's what I'm talking about. Things should be amazing. Important. Not just okay. After seeing my parents being *okay* all those years and then divorcing, I'm thinking, why wait? Why draw out a relationship if you don't think it's going anywhere?

"And you know Steve," Trisha went on, giving Leslie a little push to keep walking. "He feels things so intensely. It's kind of scary. I just want to have fun."

Suddenly Leslie felt that a great weight had been lifted from her shoulders, a weight she hadn't even realized was there. She'd been thinking something for the past week or so

. . . something she'd keep pushing to the back of her mind, never letting the thought really surface. Now it rose without anything to hold it back: Steve still liked her. More than liked her, maybe.

Lately it seemed Steve was always scrambling to be near her, in the cafeteria, in the library — even when she was in the middle of Rick's group of friends. He could still have feelings for her. Maybe he even asked Trisha out just to get to her.

"Well," Leslie began, not certain what to say to Trisha on the subject.

Then, suddenly, someone grabbed her arm and twisted it from behind.

Chapter 8

Leslie whirled around. "Steve!" she breathed, staring right into his dark, brooding eyes.

Steve clutched her arm tightly. She could feel his nails dig into her skin. His eyes darted to Trisha, then back to Leslie.

"I need to talk to Trish," he hissed, dropping her arm.

Leslie backed away, rubbing the sore spot.

"Sorry," Steve said brusquely. Then, seeming to collect himself, his expression grew calm, his voice softer.

"I am sorry, Leslie. I just really need to be alone with Trisha now."

"Sure, sure," Leslie said quickly. She shifted her eyes to Trisha, who nodded.

"Is it okay about Flamingo's? You going yourself?" Trisha spoke calmly, as if her boyfriend acted like a maniac every day of the week.

"Sure. It's just a few blocks away. It's fine. So . . ." Leslie trailed off, unsure how to continue. "I'll see you guys later," she added, trying to keep it light. Normal.

With a wave of her hand, Leslie blended in with the crowd. She couldn't resist stealing a backward glance, though, and saw Steve bend anxiously over Trisha. He didn't look half as fierce as he had a moment before.

Maybe Steve really does care about Trisha, Leslie thought, more confused than ever. Maybe he knows she wants to break up and is so torn apart, he's not thinking clearly.

Mulling everything over as she left the mall, Leslie walked slowly to the restaurant. By the time she approached the plush red carpet by the entrance, Leslie decided their breakup was all for the best. What if Steve grew even more intense, more driven? He'd just drag Trisha down further, and she certainly didn't need that.

In fact, Trisha had probably been thinking about breaking up for a while. That would account for her bad temper the past few weeks, those digs at Leslie, who was happily dating a nice normal guy. She'd been edgy about Steve, as well as her parents.

Still, Leslie couldn't help feeling bad for Steve. She'd known him a long time. They'd been through a lot together, and she hated to see him hurt or rejected.

Again.

The whole thing was so confusing! Leslie hurried the last few steps to the restaurant, looking forward to thinking about something simple and good. Her Sweet Sixteen dinner at Flamingo's.

"What do you mean?" Leslie said ten minutes later, trying to understand the maitre d'. "My reservation has been canceled?" Her voice rose at the end of the sentence, turning shrill. She knew she sounded young, like a bratty little girl who wasn't getting her way.

The maitre d', a tall man with a hook nose, nodded.

"Are you sure? That's Barrows with a B. For May eleventh."

"I told you, we have a wedding scheduled that day."

Leslie squinted in the dimly lit restaurant. Behind her, pink flamingo statues perched in a fountain, balancing on one leg. Deep, dark carpet stretched through the lobby. On the verge of tears, she felt her lower lip tremble.

The whole place — the whole problem — seemed too much for one fifteen-year-old girl to handle. Leslie wished her parents were there, or at least her sister, Sharon. Someone who carried more authority.

Somehow Leslie got hold of herself, then decided to head back home. Her other errands could wait. She needed to rest, unwind.

The bus ride home wound through Medvale, taking Leslie past the high school, the mall, and familiar tree-lined streets. Focusing on the comforting sights, Leslie took deep breaths and tried to stay calm.

"Everything will work out," she told herself. "If I can't have the dinner at Flamingo's, I'll just find somewhere else. It's certainly not the end of the world. It's just another case of bad luck."

Convincing herself that all was well, Leslie stepped off the bus at her corner. She strolled up the block, soaking in the warm spring sunshine.

"I'm home," she called as she opened the front door and dropped her knapsack. No one answered.

Leslie checked the refrigerator door for messages and found a note from her parents, held fast by a kitchen magnet. They'd gone out for dinner.

P.S. the note said, *a friend of yours left a message on our answering machine. We saved it for you.*

A friend? If it was Rick or Deborah or Trisha — or anyone her parents knew — they would have mentioned the friend by name. Curious, Leslie punched the message button on the machine on the kitchen counter.

Instantly she heard a strangely familiar voice. "I just got my invitation to your party," the girl was saying. "And I can't wait. I'll be the first to arrive and the last to leave! Just try and stop me."

The girl sounded more threatening than excited, and then she laughed. A high-pitched, squeaky laugh that sent Leslie's head spinning.

Caroline! Somehow, some way, she'd gotten an invitation!

Chapter 9

Leslie stood stock-still in the middle of the kitchen. First the cute little ice-skate invitations had disappeared. Then the restaurant reservation was mysteriously canceled. Now, Leslie thought, Caroline — crazy Caroline — is going to be at my Sweet Sixteen?

Why is everything going wrong?

Leslie grabbed a diet Coke from the refrigerator. Then she put it back. She opened up a kitchen cabinet, then slammed it shut. She didn't know what to do with herself. She felt like she had all this excess energy. It stemmed from anger. And she might as well put it to good use, she decided.

Leslie stomped up the stairs to her room. She flung open the door to her closet, and set to reorganizing it with a vengeance. Tossing clothes she hadn't worn since eighth grade in one corner, her mind raced with everything that had been going on.

"All these bad things are just a coincidence," she muttered. "They have to be."

An old Chutes and Ladders board game . . . her rock collection, or the beginnings of one. Just a plastic bag filled with odd-shaped stones. She threw them all to another corner.

Bit by bit, Leslie began to calm down. She was sorting out her thoughts along with her closet.

"Everything that happened is just a coincidence. Bad luck. A rotten bad-luck coincidence."

Suddenly she pictured Trisha, distraught as she tried to hide her horrible new haircut. The image flashed through Leslie's mind and stayed there, turning up again and again like a bad penny.

Another picture bubbled to the surface. Trisha fingering her earlobes, telling Leslie about the missing silver earrings.

Bad luck. Bad luck. Both she and Trisha had been having a string of it.

Leslie sat back on her heels, abandoning her still messy closet. Not too much longer now, and she and Trisha would be turning sixteen. Their birthdays were just around the corner.

Grave trouble. You'll have grave trouble be-
fore your sixteenth birthdays.

Feeling faint, Leslie slumped against the closet door, her eyes open but unseeing.

It's all coming true, she thought. Just like Mrs. Krashmer predicted!

Leslie jumped up to pace around her room. She began to speak out loud, unable to keep her thoughts bottled up.

"No," she protested, shaking her head. "You're just being superstitious again. These things have to be a coincidence.

"And all this stuff that happened? It isn't close to 'grave trouble.' Besides, who knows if Caroline got an invitation at all? Maybe she's just trying to bluff her way into going . . . into messing up my party."

Not knowing what else to do. Leslie leaned forward to tackle the closet once again. She reached into its dark recesses. Her fingers closed around something hard. Was it some kind of textbook buried under all her clothes?

"Granny's old photo album!" Leslie exclaimed, pulling out an old, frayed book.

What was it doing there? Why wasn't it with the rest of Granny's things in the attic?

No matter, Leslie decided, already feeling better. She'd just look through the photos. She'd gain some perspective on her problems by seeing how Granny got through rough times. After all, what were a few botched arrangements for one Sweet Sixteen?

Leslie scooted over to her bed. Sighing with pleasure, she flipped open the album. The first picture she saw was Granny and Mrs. Krashmer. It was an old black-and-white photo, and the friends were posed on a park bench somewhere. The two women looked troubled. Unnerved by whatever they were seeing. A wild wind whipped their hair straight behind them and lightning lit the sky. The date: April 28.

April 28? That was today!

Leslie let the cover fall back down, her stomach flipping with anxiety.

What were the chances she'd discover the photo album today, of all days? What did it mean? That these weren't just coincidences? That the prediction was coming true?

"This can't be a sign," she told herself. "It can't be!"

The women's troubled expressions, the growing storm behind them meant nothing. How could it?

Still, Leslie wanted reassurance. She needed reassurance. Whom could she call? Someone who would understand. Someone who'd be just as affected by it all. She hesitated just a second. Then, standing shakily, she reached for the phone by her bed.

"Trisha," she said when her cousin answered, "I have to tell you something."

Quickly Leslie explained about Flamingo's, Caroline, the photo album, and her crazy idea that the whole thing was related to Mrs. Krashmer's prediction. "I know I'm being nutty," she explained. "But I can't shake this creepy feeling that Mrs. Krashmer was right."

Trisha was silent for a moment. Leslie could hear her breath coming in short, shallow gulps.

"Come on," Leslie tried to joke. "Aren't you going to say it's time for the men in white coats to take me away? That I'm imagining things? Or," she said, sounding more serious, "that at least I'm blowing things out of proportion?"

"Okay," Trisha said slowly.

"That's all you're going to say? Okay? That doesn't mean anything."

Trisha gave a short laugh. "Okay, you're blowing things out of proportion."

Leslie shifted the phone to her other ear. "You don't sound very convincing."

"The whole idea is crazy," Trisha said more firmly. "It's just . . ."

Leslie sat up straighter. "What? What?"

"Well, you know how I planned to break up with Steve."

Leslie groaned. "I forgot all about that. I'm sorry, Trisha. How did it go?"

"In a word? Rotten. As in just my rotten luck, I picked today of all days. The day when Steve heard back about that internship he applied for his senior year. You know, to work at the university for school credit?"

Leslie groaned again. "Let me guess. He didn't get it."

"Bingo!" Trisha said drily. "And I guess he's been relying on me more than I realized. All along I thought he was more into the relationship than I was. But I didn't know how much."

"So what happened?"

"He flipped out. I've never seen him so upset. He stalked around the mall, dragging me behind him, saying he'll never let me go. His face turned this weird shade of red. I mean, he was really crazed.

"So you see," she wound up, "that kind of falls under Mrs. Krashmer's prediction, too."

Did it? Leslie didn't think so. Sure it was bad luck that Trisha had chosen today to talk to Steve. But she had made that decision. It wasn't pure blind luck. Or even really chance. Leslie was beginning to see things more rationally.

"Listen, Trisha," Leslie began. "We're both

being silly here. Let's stop and think this through clearly." She was just about to go on, when the doorbell rang.

"Let me call you back," she told her cousin. Then she hurried downstairs, trying to catch a glimpse of the caller through the front-door window.

It was a man; someone in an official-looking brown uniform. Were her parents expecting some kind of delivery?

Leslie opened the door, noting the delivery truck — Parson's Speedy Delivery — parked in the driveway. "Yes," she said to the man. He held a flat box wrapped with brown paper. "May I help you?"

The man flipped through some pages on his clipboard. "Delivery for L. Barrows," he told her.

"I'm L. Barr — I mean Leslie Barrows. But I'm not expecting a delivery."

"From Fiona's?"

"Oh." Leslie grinned. "I did buy something there."

Not just something — the dress for her Sweet Sixteen dinner. Her beautiful dark velvet dress that swirled around her ankles like soft, gentle waves.

"But it wasn't supposed to be delivered. I was going to pick it up."

The man shrugged, holding out the box.

"I guess it doesn't make a difference," Leslie said, suddenly glad it was there. "I guess they got the dress in earlier than they expected."

For once, things were going her way. Leslie signed the delivery sheet, thanked the delivery man, then shut the door — still smiling.

Eager to see the dress, she tore open the box. Carefully, she lifted the smooth black velvet from the tissue paper.

Leslie gasped. Her fingers were sliding through the luxurious material, poking through the dress as if it were made of Swiss cheese.

Her beautiful formal dress! It was slashed to ribbons.

Chapter 10

The next morning, Leslie woke before her alarm went off. She cast her eyes around the still-dark room, stopping when she reached the ripped-up dress hanging on the back of her chair.

She'd have to bring it back to the store. Explain that she received it damaged. The dress hung awkwardly, one sleeve twisted at a strange angle, the ribbons of material swirling around the chair legs. For a moment, Leslie had a vision of herself in the dress, her arm twisted, the cuts of the dress matching the cuts on —

Stop it! she told herself. You're scaring yourself. This is just a mistake. Damaged goods get sent out all the time. All you have to do is return it.

Leslie stood up, slipping her feet into fluffy slippers. She shuffled across the floor, not paying attention to where she was walking.

"Oof!" she cried, stumbling on her grandmother's photo album. Suddenly she remembered the dream she'd just awakened from. Every little bit of it, as if it were a movie, unfolding right before her eyes.

Leslie was young, no more than five or six. She was sitting on her grandmother's lap.

"Hush, hush, child," Granny whispered as she gently brushed Leslie's long red hair. She smiled softly, leaning forward to tell Leslie a secret. A secret that would make a difference when she grew older. . . . A secret that could change her life.

It was —

The phone rang. And just like that, the dream faded to nothingness.

"Now I'll never remember," Leslie thought as she picked up the phone.

"Hello?"

"Listen, Les, I'm sorry to call now. I know it's really early."

"Rick?" Leslie smiled, flopping back on her bed. "I don't mind. It's kind of nice hearing your voice first thing in the morning. And last thing at night," she added. "Thanks for listening to all my problems for hours on end."

After Leslie had opened the dress box, she had called Trisha back and told her what happened. Then she'd phoned Rick, knowing he'd be sympathetic. And he had been wonderful: caring, concerned.

Not every guy would understand about a ruined dress, she'd thought.

Now Rick cleared his throat. "Listen," he said again. "I can't take you to school this morning."

Rick's voice sounded strained. A little hurried and nervous. Slowly Leslie sat up. "What's up?" she asked, keeping her tone level.

"Oh, it's really nothing. Just some errands."

"Errands? At seven A.M.?" Leslie couldn't keep from sounding suspicious. She pictured Caroline sending Rick on some fool's errand — like finding chocolate-covered strawberries before the stores even opened — and him perfectly willing to do it.

"I'll make it up to you, Les. I promise." Rick lowered his voice, half-whispering. "You know I'd do anything for you. This doesn't mean a thing. You can count on me for anything."

Neither of them had mentioned Caroline. Yet somehow, that's who they were discussing, and they both knew it.

"All right," Leslie told him. "But I've got to go. If I'm going to take the bus, I need to get ready now."

They said good-bye quickly, the tension eased but not totally erased. Leslie checked the clock. She'd really better hurry, if she wanted to catch the bus.

The dirty, creaky old school bus. She hadn't been on it since she and Rick started dating. She could picture it easily, though. All the freshman kids crowded on board, shouting, laughing. None of her new friends — the cool older ones — ever rode the bus.

Quickly, Leslie dialed Deborah. As her fingers punched the familiar numbers, Leslie felt a twinge of doubt. Had she gotten so used to being chauffeured around, she couldn't bear a simple bus ride?

Am I too dependent on Rick? she wondered. Am I as bad as Caroline?

Leslie started to hang up the phone, but Deborah was already saying, "Hello? Hello?" And an hour later, Leslie climbed into the front seat of the Shaw family station wagon.

"Thanks," she told Deborah. "I know this is short notice."

"Hey, don't worry about it," Deborah said, turning out of Leslie's driveway. "It's fun to have a full car."

"A full car? Who else are you taking?"

"Trisha." Deborah faced Leslie briefly, her expression a mix of emotions. "You know we went to get our hair cut yesterday."

Yesterday? Was it only yesterday? So much had happened!

Leslie nodded, careful not to say anything about the haircut or how it happened.

"Well, I felt so bad about Trisha — you know it was my idea for her to get a haircut? — I called last night to see how she was doing. She told me she broke up with Steve."

"I know," Leslie put in.

"You do?" Deborah seemed disappointed that Trisha had confided in Leslie as well. "Well, anyway," she continued, "Steve obviously isn't driving her to school anymore. So I offered!"

They pulled in front of Trisha's house and Trisha ran out, her hair pulled back with a headband.

"It looks good that way," Leslie said as Trisha ducked into the backseat.

"So you think I could pass for a normal teenager?" Trisha joked as Deborah drove off.

Leslie noticed Trisha's eyes were swollen. From crying last night, she'd bet, upset about Steve.

"Maybe not normal," Leslie teased a little tentatively. She turned to see how Trisha took the joke, and was glad to see her cousin smiling back.

Even Deborah had a grin plastered on her face. An almost self-satisfied grin.

"So here we are," she announced merrily. "Three single chicks cruising the streets on the way to school."

Leslie cleared her throat.

"Of course you have a boyfriend, Les," Deborah said. "But you never know. I mean, here you are driving with me, while Rick is probably pouring milk into Caroline's cereal for her. Things haven't been going so great for you lately. For either of you lately," she added, nodding at Trisha.

There was that self-satisfied grin again, Leslie couldn't help noticing.

"You know," Deborah was saying as she turned into the school parking lot. "I just saw a talk show about boyfriends on the rebound. A psychologist was on, saying how guys are most vulnerable when they've been dumped. Although I don't think she actually said 'dumped.' I think she used the word 'rejected.'"

Deborah laughed. "Maybe I should try for Steve now. He's been double-dumped. Easy prey, I'd say."

Trisha laughed, too. But Leslie had the sneaking feeling that Deborah was partly serious. Thinking back, she realized Deborah's face always colored slightly when she saw Steve, and she did seem to mention him a lot, trying to bring his name into the conversation.

With a shock, Leslie realized Deborah liked Steve. She'd probably liked him all along. And she'd been acting funny lately, not just because she felt left out of Leslie's new life, but because she missed Leslie's old boyfriend, too.

Leslie tried to picture the two together. Serious-minded Steve watching Oprah with Deborah, munching on snacks and comparing Oprah's panelists with Phil's, Montel's, and Sally Jessy's. Laughing about *Snob Central*.

No, she couldn't quite see it.

Oh Deb, she thought, be careful. Steve's not the only one who's vulnerable.

Still thinking it over later, Leslie caught sight of Steve in the school hallway. He balanced an armload of books while navigating the crowded corridor, his forehead creased in concentration.

"Steve?" she said quietly.

Steve jerked his head to face her.

"I'm sorry," she said haltingly.

"Just what are you sorry about?" he asked, his eyes hooded, his voice low.

She couldn't say she was sorry about Trisha dumping him. Leslie knew it would come out all wrong; all pitying and insincere. It would only make him feel even worse.

"I — I — I heard you didn't get the university internship," she stuttered.

Steve shrugged. "It's okay. It turns out I wasn't crazy about the idea anyway."

Steve's eyes focused on hers finally, and they seemed to penetrate clear through to her brain. "I'd miss too many things here."

He bent closer, gazing at her intently. Then he reached down to touch her cheek. Turning on his heel, he left Leslie standing alone in the now empty hall.

Not quite empty, Leslie realized, whirling around as a locker door slammed shut.

Deborah had witnessed the whole thing.

Chapter 11

Blackness enveloped her like a silky down quilt. Leslie had the feeling she was swimming effortlessly through a midnight sky. Carried by gentle winds. Rested. Buoyant.

The darkness drew in closer. The air felt heavier. Leslie squirmed, suddenly uneasy. The blackness covered her like a shroud now; like a close-fitting veil wrapped tight around her body. Dragging, pulling, pushing her down. She heard a door slam shut.

Leslie coughed. She flailed her arms wildly, and hit something solid.

A closet. She was in a closet. A small tight closet with no hope of escaping. No hope of living. Her breath came in gasps as the heaviness pressed in. Closer, closer, weighing her down. Clogging her nose and her throat. Smothering —

"Ahhh!" Leslie woke up, choking. She

bolted upright, her hands on her throat, not quite believing it hadn't been real.

"A dream," she whispered. "That's all it was. A nightmare."

She was sweating, still breathing hard. Leslie pushed back her hair with one shaky hand. The other gripped her bedpost, anchoring her in reality. A heaviness seemed to settle around her . . . a heaviness like the dream.

A dream is just a dream, Leslie told herself later, as she dressed for school. Put it out of your mind.

But for some reason, that strange uneasy feeling stayed with her like an unwelcome visitor. She couldn't shake it — not during the ride to school or in her early classes.

It was as if the darkness — the suffocating closeness of it all — lurked around every corner, waiting to claim her once again.

By lunchtime, Leslie had finally begun to settle down — until Rick came up from behind to give her a hug. "You're kind of jumpy today," Rick said when Leslie flinched. "Is everything okay?"

Leslie nodded. She didn't want to tell anyone about the nightmare. It would just summon up the terror. It would just sink her back into darkness.

All morning long, she'd been thinking the

nightmare had something to do with Mrs. Krashmer . . . with her prediction . . . just like the other dream, the one with her grandmother telling her a secret. She didn't know why. She just had a feeling. It was a sign — like finding the photo album with that strange picture. It meant the fortune was coming true.

The darkness. The cold, smothering darkness.

Grave trouble could hit any time. Any instant. From any angle.

Right now, right here in school.

But nothing happened. Nothing at all. And by the time she sat next to Trisha in study hall, the day was practically over. Leslie felt almost safe. Things aren't as bad as all that, she decided.

After all, Fiona's had agreed to replace the dress when she explained what happened. They said she had requested that the dress be delivered — or at least that's what they had on record. But Leslie figured it was just a mix-up.

Even better, Leslie had gotten a phone call from the maitre d' at Flamingo's, saying he had tried to call the bride who'd reserved the dining room, but he'd gotten a tow-truck company. He checked the phone book, but she wasn't listed. So as far as he was concerned, she didn't even exist. The restaurant was Leslie's for the eleventh.

Practically everything had been fixed. The reservation, the dress, the invitations. Sure, Caroline was still coming to her Sweet Sixteen, or threatening to. But maybe that wouldn't be so bad either.

So why was she fixated on the prediction and the dream?

Leslie turned to her cousin, about to blurt out the whole horrid nightmare. Who else could she confide in? Who else wouldn't laugh and spread the word that Leslie Barrows was slowly but surely losing her marbles?

But Trisha was in a good mood. A great mood, really. She sat at her desk, humming loudly as she doodled happily in her notebook, oblivious to the teacher's stern looks. And considering how upset Trisha had been over Steve and the haircut, Leslie didn't want to spoil it.

At a table behind them, Caroline snickered with Donna. They'd been at it for the past half hour now, getting noisier and noisier. Leslie knew she was their prime topic of conversation. She could feel two sets of eyes bore into her back. Two tongues wagging all about her — about the ruined dress, the reservations. These things had a way of getting around.

Leslie sighed, feeling cast adrift from any

group. Things were changing, and where did she belong? With Rick and his friends? Leslie snorted. Maybe with Rick, but his friends were still one big question mark, thanks to Caroline. Donna had been nice to her over the weekend, sure. But Donna's best friend, Caroline, hadn't been around.

And then there were Deborah and Steve. Who knew if she'd ever feel comfortable with either one of them again? How could she get back that easy familiarity? That solid friendship?

Strange, Leslie thought, I'm beginning to feel closest to Trisha out of everyone.

Sitting next to Leslie, Trisha bent toward her notebook. A dreamy smile played around the corners of her mouth as she shaded in a piece of the paper.

"You look like you just won the lottery," Leslie whispered. "What's going on?"

Trisha pushed over her notebook so Leslie could see the picture. It was a stick figure wearing ice skates and an elaborately drawn skating outfit. The outfit looked like a redone tuxedo, complete with a vest, jacket, and a short pleated skirt.

"Isn't this the coolest thing you've ever seen?" asked Trisha. "It's a white tuxedo. I saw it in the Blades catalog, and when I told my mom about it, she said I should buy it."

Trisha smoothed down her jeans, as if she already wore the skirt. "Mom's talked things over with my dad. And he agreed I should definitely have a new outfit to wear to your party! And," she continued, "I might have a Sweet Sixteen, too!"

"Hey! That's terrific!" Leslie's voice rose with excitement, and she caught the eye of Ms. Hawkins, the teacher. She quickly poked her nose back in a book, but she couldn't stop grinning. Trisha had just been pretending not to care about clothes or money or a Sweet Sixteen, but it had really meant something. Leslie felt glad for Trisha. And, she had to admit, a little happy for herself, too.

Now *this* is a sign, she thought. A sign that things are turning around. The bad streak is over. For both of us.

Caroline suddenly dropped a book to the floor. It landed with a deliberate bang, and Donna giggled loudly.

"Girls!" The teacher stalked over to their general area, her finger wagging. "I don't want to have to tell you again. Please be quiet."

"Leslie," Trisha said under her breath when Ms. Hawkins had walked away. "Can you come over after school? My skating outfit is being delivered. I want you to be there when I try it on."

"Okay. But let's get some pizza first." An image from her dream flashed before her eyes — darkness. A door slamming shut. "I haven't been able to eat all day, and now I'm starving."

"Ms. Hawkins!" Caroline raised her hand. Leslie swiveled, the queasy, uneasy feeling coming back.

Ms. Hawkins tiptoed close to their tables. "Yes, dear?"

"There's so much talking in here, I can't concentrate." Caroline sounded distressed. Sincere. And she was looking pointedly at Leslie.

Ms. Hawkins's mouth turned down in an angry line. "Of course, dear." She turned to face Leslie and Trisha. "I will not abide talking during study hall. Is that clear? One more time and you'll find yourselves in detention."

Mutely, Leslie nodded. She'd never been talked to that way by a teacher before. She'd never been in any sort of trouble.

Leslie felt her face flush, as all eyes in the room seemed to focus right on her. She heard a chair scrape the floor behind her, then someone walking softly to the pencil sharpener. It was Caroline. Her eyes flashed at Leslie as she put one finger to her lips, then mouthed the word "detention."

Leslie felt like screaming. Like shouting that Caroline had been talking louder than anyone. She should be the one in trouble; the one to get detention.

But what could she do?

"Caroline's a witch."

Leslie and Trisha were walking to Trisha's house from the bus stop, and Trisha was offering her opinion. "You know how to get back at her? How to make her really crazy? Just ignore her."

The afternoon sun warmed Leslie, easing her tension and helping her relax. A Frisbee sailed through the air, landing at her feet. Leslie picked it up and tossed it back to two boys playing in a front yard.

"I've already thought of that. I just wish Rick would ignore her, too," Leslie said, joking feebly.

"They do have a strange relationship," Trisha agreed as they walked up her driveway and into her house. "I can't figure out if Caroline is completely nuts, or if Rick enjoys having her —

"Oh look!" she cried, interrupting herself to grab a package from the table in the front hall.

"It's here! My tuxedo outfit! Mom must have signed for it before she left for work."

Trisha hurried into the living room, clutching the box tightly. "Wait till you see it," she told Leslie over her shoulder. "You won't believe it."

Leslie followed behind. "I've never seen you like this, Trisha. You're like a kid with a new bike."

Trisha tore open the package. Brown paper wrapping flew over the living room, sinking to the floor like confetti. "I do feel like a little kid, and it's my birthday and Christmas all combined."

Trisha grinned as she shook the plain white box with BLADES lettered on top. "Gee," she said, laughing. "I wonder what it is." Her grin growing wide, she lifted the box cover.

Leslie sidled closer, trying to get a peek at the tuxedo. All she could see was tissue paper. "Let me see," she said, peering around Trisha.

But Trisha stood blocking her way. Her grin froze in place like a grisly mask. Still as a statue, her eyes darted around the room as if she didn't know where to look.

"Quit fooling around," Leslie said. "Hold out the outfit."

Finally, Trisha moved. She dropped the box

as if it were a red-hot coal. Then she turned and ran out of the room.

"Trisha?" Leslie called. What was going on? Was Trisha playing some kind of practical joke?

Leslie stooped down to peer inside the box. The tissue paper still covered everything, so she pushed it aside.

Digging deeper into the box, Leslie felt something wet. Sticky.

With a gasp, Leslie pulled back her arm. Her fingers were stained a deep bright red. The kind of red you see in hospital emergency rooms. At auto accidents. The kind of red that could be only one thing.

Not quite believing her eyes, Leslie ripped away the rest of the tissue paper. And there was the white tuxedo outfit.

Smeared with blood from top to bottom.

Chapter 12

"Trisha?" Leslie knocked softly on Trisha's bedroom door. "Are you okay?"

Trisha answered with a muffled reply, so Leslie swung open the door. Her head under the pillow, her body shaking with silent sobs, Trisha lay curled like a kitten on her bed.

Hesitantly Leslie stepped closer, then stroked Trisha's back.

"It's not blood," she said softly. "It's paint. Red paint."

"What?" Trisha sat up, her faced streaked with tears.

"The tuxedo. There's paint all over it." Leslie held her fingers near Trisha's nose. Trisha sniffed, and a look of confusion passed over her face.

"Oh, I thought . . ." Trisha trailed off. Her voice lifted hopefully. "Do you think it will come off?"

Leslie shook her head. "It's almost all dry now."

"But we can try!"

Trisha jumped off her bed, then raced into the living room. She grabbed the tuxedo, then tossed it into the kitchen sink. Turning on the water full blast, she emptied the bottle of dishwashing liquid before Leslie could stop her.

"Trisha!" Leslie shouted, hurrying into the kitchen. "You're just going to make it worse."

Leslie lifted the outfit out of the sink. Already the paint had run, staining even more of the white material.

Trisha sagged against the counter. "I give up."

Leslie reached over to turn off the water. Then she led Trisha over to the table and gently pushed her into a chair.

"Listen. It must be some horrible mistake. Maybe the warehouse was being painted and some of the merchandise got in the way. I've ordered stuff from the Blades catalog. The staff is really nice. We'll tell them what happened. They'll exchange the outfit. I know they will. Fiona's did it for me."

Fiona's. Her beautiful velvet dress in tatters. The invitations, lost. The reservations, bungled. The haircut. The earrings. The frightening dreams, that somehow tied in to everything. Leslie ticked off the incidents, one by one.

And now this.

As if reading her thoughts, Trisha sighed. "Grave trouble. Seems we've been having a lot of it lately."

They'd never gotten around to discussing Mrs. Krashmer's prediction the other night on the phone, what with Leslie's dress being delivered, and Trisha breaking up with Steve. Now the two girls faced each other with one thing on their minds: Was the fortune coming true?

"I'm not sure," Trisha said slowly. "I hate to blame everything on one silly prediction from years ago. I've been doing a lot of thinking about this. At first, you know, I was ready to believe it. Eager to believe it, really. I wanted to put all the blame — all the responsibility for things going haywire — on something. Anything — even our fortunes coming true. But then I realized something. Bad things happen all the time." She looked away as she added, "Divorce. Breakups. That's life. And it doesn't have anything to do with any prediction."

"But Trisha," Leslie argued, convinced they had cause to worry more than ever. "All these things that are happening *now*? You can't ignore them! I know I go overboard sometimes with the superstitious stuff. And some things are getting straightened out. But I'm not just being paranoid. The incidents are growing worse."

Trisha slowly turned back to Leslie. And when she spoke her voice was tinged with scorn — almost like the old Trisha. "I suppose you think Mrs. Krashmer knows all the answers."

"That's it!" Leslie paced the kitchen floor, her voice rising with excitement. "I want to find Mrs. Krashmer. I want to talk to her, find out more. Maybe there's a way to stop these things from happening. Maybe she'd know!"

Leslie felt a rush of hope. She'd been talking off the top of her head, letting random thoughts guide her words. But now she began to believe what she said. Mrs. Krashmer held the key to all their problems.

"Help me find her," she pleaded.

Trisha wrung out her sopping tuxedo, then tossed it on the floor. "You sound so desperate, I guess I'll have to." She smiled uneasily, uncertainly. "I don't think it's going to lead anywhere. But you win. Where do we begin?"

A few hours later, Leslie and Trisha sat in the back of a local bus. Bouncing on the hard plastic seats, they looked out the window as they rode through Old Town, a rundown area on the outskirts of Medvale.

It hadn't taken them long to find Mrs. Krashmer's address. They'd searched Leslie's attic for Granny's old trunk, then found a tattered address book tucked into a corner.

Leslie had flipped through the brittle pages excitedly, stopping at K and pointing at the last entry on the page. Krashmer.

"There's no phone number," she'd said, disappointed. "I'll bet she doesn't even have a telephone. But we can figure out where the address is on the map."

Now, consulting the map on the bus, Leslie glanced up at a passing street sign. "Let's get off at the next stop. Grand Street must be around here somewhere."

The two girls clambered down the bus steps a moment later. Then they stood in the street, gazing around.

Clearly, the neighborhood had once been imposing. The richest families in Medvale used to live there, in large, ornate houses with lush lawns and great elm trees branching overhead. But the large houses had become rundown, then were broken up into apartments. Weeds had choked overgrown lawns. The elm trees had withered with neglect. Small, squat apartment buildings sprang up between the once-great homes.

Leslie had never been to Old Town before. A strange uneasiness settled in her stomach. It was dusk, and it seemed as though everyone in the neighborhood had gathered in the growing gloom — just to watch the girls walk down the street. The people looked as old as the houses. They all wore baggy, dark clothes, and sat facing the street in broken-down lawn chairs.

"Let's hurry," Trisha whispered.

Leslie nodded. "Grand Street is up ahead."

They moved quickly up the block, looking straight ahead to avoid the curious glances. Making a left onto Grand Street, they finally spied Mrs. Krashmer's house.

Trisha stood close to Leslie inside the front door as she rang the bell marked KRASHMER. A heavyset woman, her hair in a scarf, slowly made her way down the steep stairs to the entryway.

"Hello?" she called down in a thick accent.

"Mrs. Krashmer?" Leslie asked in the fading light.

The woman laughed hollowly. "Mrs. Krashmer doesn't live here anymore."

Up close, Leslie could see the woman wasn't Mrs. Krashmer — it was only her clothes and voice that made Leslie think she was Granny's friend.

"Do you know where she is?" Leslie asked. "Where we can find her?"

Again, the woman laughed. "Sure. The Merry Glades Nursing Home. She moved there about a year ago."

Before Leslie could ask anything else, the woman shut the door and disappeared into the dark corridor. Trisha stepped outside, holding the door open for Leslie to follow.

"I remember passing the nursing home on the bus," she said. "It's only a few blocks from here. We can walk it."

Hurrying down the street with Trisha at her side, Leslie felt glad they were together. Doing this alone would have been tough. A little frightening.

Evening turned to night as the girls approached the Merry Glades Nursing Home.

"It certainly doesn't look very merry," Trisha said, stopping in front. The old stone building loomed in front of them. Heavy wooden doors blocked the entrance. Ivy crept along the walls. Iron bars covered long windows.

For a moment Leslie thought uneasily about Rick. He'd never have let her come to Old Town on a wild goose chase like this. He would have insisted on driving, escorting her around as if *she* were ready for the nursing home.

But now, Leslie began to wish for Rick's solid, comforting presence.

"Well, we've come all this way," Leslie said, pushing against the door. "We can't turn back because of one scary old nursing home."

The door creaked open. A dark, tiled corridor stretched before them, and a sharp medicinal smell slapped them in the face.

"Come on." Leslie pointed down the hall. "There's a reception desk over there."

"I'm sure we'll get quite the reception," Trisha hissed under her breath.

Leslie stifled a nervous giggle. They approached the desk, which blocked the rest of the corridor, and Leslie guessed the rest of the nursing home as well. She smiled cautiously at the receptionist.

The woman eyed them suspiciously. "May I help you?"

"We're looking for Mrs. Krashmer," Leslie explained.

"She died," the woman said shortly, her expression unchanged.

"Oh." Leslie was speechless, torn between surprise, sympathy — and disappointment. They'd come all this way for nothing. She'd been pinning all her hopes on Mrs. Krashmer

. . . on her explaining the problems away or helping them out. And now . . .

"Can you tell us a little more?" Trisha asked reasonably. "When did Mrs. Krashmer die?"

"Last week."

Leslie groaned. Why didn't she think to come sooner?

"Did she have friends here? People who knew her?" Leslie asked. She was clutching at straws, thinking maybe — just maybe — Mrs. Krashmer had confided in someone about the cousins . . . about the fortune she'd told.

The receptionist shook her head firmly. "The other residents are very disturbed over her death. I'm afraid I can't allow you to speak to anyone."

An elderly woman wearing a faded blue robe shuffled quietly behind the desk. Her bloodshot eyes peered at them from beneath dirty gray bangs. Her tangled hair hung down her back in knots. Her features looked painted on with bright-colored makeup.

"Do you know why the residents are disturbed?" she cackled.

"Hush," the receptionist said. "You don't know what you're saying."

"Of course I do!" the old woman snapped. "Mrs. Krashmer predicted her own death. That's why we're disturbed!"

PART THREE

May 1996

Chapter 13

Leslie was sitting in history class, a rapt expression on her face while she pretended to listen to Mr. Corr. It was the day after she and Trisha had visited Merry Glades Nursing Home, and Leslie was going over everything they'd learned.

Mrs. Krashmer died at the stroke of midnight, April 24. Or maybe, Leslie thought, if it's midnight, that means it's really April 23.

If she couldn't pin down the date, maybe Mrs. Krashmer didn't predict her own death. Maybe she didn't get it right at all.

Leslie sighed, knowing she was twisting things around to soothe her own frayed nerves. What difference did the date really make? Mrs. Krashmer had told everyone she'd die at the stroke of midnight. Under a full moon. In her sleep. And she did.

At least she died painlessly, Leslie thought.

Her heart went out to the old woman who died alone, away from her native land, in a sterile, unfriendly place like Merry Glades.

Above her head, Mr. Corr droned on about World War II battles. People's eyes glazed over and Leslie sank even deeper into thought.

When Leslie heard that Mrs. Krashmer predicted her own death, a cold stab of fear had shot straight through her body. She shuddered now, just picturing the odd old woman. But moments after they'd heard the news, Trisha had shrugged, convinced her death meant nothing at all. Who could believe that crazy old woman, anyway?

"Come on, Les." Trisha had shaken her head, unbelievingly. "That woman had on fake eyelashes, tons and tons of makeup, but she didn't wash her hair? I don't think she's in her right mind."

Then she'd urged Leslie not to breathe a word of this to anyone they knew. The whole thing was just too crazy.

"Who believes in fortunes?" she'd said. "No one but you."

Fortunes, fortunes, fortunes. The word rang in Leslie's head, taking up all her concentration. In her mind's eye, she saw Mrs. Krashmer lean over a teacup, her voice filled with doom. *Grave trouble before your sixteenth birthdays.*

A heavy hand suddenly descended on her shoulder. Leslie jumped in her seat, startled. Slowly, deliberately, Mr. Corr lifted his hand. But he stayed rooted to his spot, towering over her like a vulture.

Behind her, Caroline squeaked with pleasure.

Twisting her head around, Leslie noticed that Caroline was waving a bunch of papers in her hand. Make that a paper, Leslie realized. As in history paper. Leslie glanced around the room. It seemed everyone had gotten his or her paper back.

Except her.

"Please see me after class," Mr. Corr said sternly.

"What? He didn't give you your paper?" Caroline whispered to Leslie in a sympathetic voice. "You poor thing. You're probably in deep, deep trouble. And here I am, with a big fat A." Caroline put on a concerned look. "And it's all thanks to your boyfriend!"

Leslie sat rigidly in her seat, refusing to give Caroline the satisfaction of a reaction.

The bell rang and Caroline snatched up her books, shaking her head. "I hate to leave you,

Les, when you need my support — and believe me, I'd truly love to stay here and listen to you get chewed out by Mr. Corr. But" — she grinned brightly — "I have a date to meet Rick at the library."

She clamped her hand over her mouth, trying to look horrified. "Oops. Did I say date?"

Caroline waved cheerily. Then she sauntered out of the room, the center of a group of laughing girls.

Slowly, Leslie extricated herself from her seat. She'd been holding herself so stiffly, she felt sore. As if she'd run a mile in five minutes flat.

The classroom was empty now. A wave of nervousness washed over Leslie as she lifted her knapsack from the floor. An after-class conference with Corr the Bore meant trouble. No doubt about it.

"Well, Ms. Barrows." Mr. Corr leaned against his desk, his mouth set in a tight straight line. "You must be wondering why I didn't return your paper."

Leslie tried to smile. "Is everything okay?" she asked shakily.

"No!" Mr. Corr straightened. He opened a desk drawer and took out a paper — Leslie's paper, with a large red F scrawled on the top.

"I'm very disappointed in you, Leslie. All year long, you did excellent work. But who knows?" Mr. Corr sighed deeply. "It could all be attributed to dishonesty, to cheating, just like this paper."

Leslie gasped. Cheating? She'd never cheated in her life. What did he mean?

"Please don't pretend you're surprised. I know for a fact you copied this paper."

Mr. Corr reached into the drawer again. He pulled out another term paper. "Someone sent me the original. I don't know who. The postmark was from another town. Warrenton. Do you have relatives there, Leslie? Did you copy this paper from an older cousin?"

Unthinkingly, Leslie grasped the paper. The whole scene didn't seem real. It couldn't be real.

"This is a mistake," she told Mr. Corr, struggling to keep calm. "There must be an explanation."

Holding the term paper between trembling fingers, Leslie gazed down at the first sheet. *Winston Churchill: The Man and the Policies*.

Leslie sucked in her breath. She felt she'd been punched in the stomach. Hard. Because underneath the title was a name. No first name. Just a last one.

But it couldn't be. It just couldn't.

Leslie's vision blurred. She blinked to clear it. And the name was still the same.

Krashmer.

Chapter 14

"Your parents will be alerted," Mr. Corr called out as Leslie stumbled from the classroom. "And there's every chance you'll fail this course."

Gasping for breath, Leslie lurched into the hallway.

How could this have happened? How could her paper be a copy?

Leslie's mind darted in different directions, trying to sort out the puzzle. But she was too distraught, too upset, to think things through. She couldn't even remember when she handed the paper in. She had to slow down. Catch her breath. But her parents! They would flip out. They'd freak. Their darling little Leslie, a liar and a cheat.

Maybe they'd cancel the Sweet Sixteen.

Leslie pressed against the wall, willing herself to concentrate. To remember who was there the day she handed in her paper. The day the invitations were stolen. She closed her eyes.

But unwelcome thoughts came crashing into her mind. Thoughts of someone out to get her. Deliberately trying to scare her. Someone who didn't want her to have a Sweet Sixteen.

Who didn't want her to have anything.

"Leslie! Leslie!" Trisha clutched her arm, forcing her to look at her. "Are you all right?"

Leslie sagged against Trisha. "I don't know," she cried. She waved the history paper in Trisha's face. "Everything is ruined."

"What? What's ruined? What is that?"

"My term paper — and a copy."

Quickly, Leslie explained what happened. As the hall slowly emptied out, Trisha listened carefully, her face draining of color.

"I have to show you something, too," she whispered.

She opened her notebook and took out a sheet of paper filled with multiple-choice questions. "It's my history test. I just got it back."

Leslie stared at the F on top, not understanding.

"Look!" Trisha insisted, holding it closer. Her hand trembled. "I failed it. But someone changed my answers."

Leslie squinted. She could make out a vague

outline of the right answers, erased and replaced with the wrong ones.

Someone had changed almost all the answers.

Leslie gripped Trisha's elbow. This was it. Proof positive that fate was stepping in to mess up their lives. That Mrs. Krashmer was right.

"Do you believe me now?" Leslie hissed. "The prediction is coming true!"

For a moment, Trisha seemed convinced. A look of fright crossed her face, and her hand shook even harder. Then she grew resolute. "Listen, Leslie. It's only some kid who wants to get the best grades in history. Practically the whole school knows about the prediction. We were just set up. That's why he or she used the name Krashmer."

Trisha pushed her short hair away from her face. "This doesn't have anything to do with those other . . . incidents," she declared. "It can't."

Touching Leslie's shoulder, Trisha spoke calmly. Convincingly. Leslie felt herself relax, her heartbeat return to normal. But she didn't agree with Trisha. Not at all.

"Maybe, maybe not," she said. She wanted to persuade Trisha to see it her way. "I'll call you later. We can talk things over. Decide what to do."

Trisha raised one eyebrow. "Do?" she repeated. "What can we do? We can't tell anyone your theory. They'd think we were nuts. The only thing to do is wait. Wait and see what happens next."

Finally Leslie agreed. If word leaked out to Caroline that she actually thought the fortune was coming true, she'd be the laughingstock of school. And forget about her brand-new social life. She could kiss it good-bye — along with Rick.

In the meantime, though, there was one thing she couldn't avoid. Telling her parents about the paper.

Surprisingly, her parents — always so concerned with education — were understanding when she talked to them later that night.

Leslie wasn't sure if they entirely believed her story about someone getting hold of her paper and playing a dirty trick on her. But they said they could see she was under a lot of pressure, what with the upcoming party, a new boyfriend, and all the end-of-term schoolwork.

Leslie would have to rewrite the history paper, of course. And from now on, no more going out on school nights. But they trusted her. And even if she had made one mistake, they felt sure it wouldn't happen again.

"You mean that's it?" Leslie said disbelievingly. "I can still have my Sweet Sixteen?"

Mr. Barrows grinned. "Sure you can. That is, if you still want it."

"I want it! I want it!" Leslie rushed over to embrace her parents in one giant hug.

Then she pulled back, filled with a sudden urge to confide in them. It was so tempting to pour out all her problems, to let her parents take over. Tell her what to do.

But she couldn't. She'd promised Trisha to keep it quiet. And what if her parents got scared by all the incidents? What if they decided to call off the party, concerned for her safety? Leslie didn't want to take the chance.

"I'm going to call Trisha," she told her parents. "Tell her the good news."

Leslie's mother patted her arm, a pleased expression on her face. "I'm so glad you two are friends. It's such a comfort to Aunt May."

Smiling, Leslie went into her bedroom to make the call. Just as she was reaching for the receiver, the phone rang.

"Hello," Leslie said, picking it up.

She heard nothing but silence.

"Hello?" Leslie said again.

A buzz of static came over the line, then quiet once again. Shrugging, Leslie reached to hang up. But she stopped short. She'd heard a click, a sound like a tape or CD being turned on.

"Happy birthday to you. Happy birthday to you . . ." A joyful chorus of children's voices sang over the wire.

"Sharon? Is that you?" Leslie asked, laughing, thinking it was her older sister calling from college.

No one answered.

"Come on, who is this?"

Still no answer.

Leslie listened carefully, hoping for some sort of clue. Slowly the childish voices rose higher and higher, as though someone changed the tape speed. Leslie jerked the phone away from her ear.

The voices grew more shrill . . . carrying through the air . . . shrieking their birthday wishes. They screamed, "How old are you now?" . . . their cries ringing in Leslie's head.

Click. The machine shut off suddenly. Leslie gripped the phone, listening to silence.

Dead silence.

Chapter 15

The shrieks and screams still pounded in her head. Leslie grasped the phone as if it were a life preserver and she was drowning. Shaking, she punched in Trisha's number.

"It's not just strange random events," Leslie told her quickly. "Or bad luck. And we didn't get those history grades because some crazy overachiever wants to be number one."

"What do you mean?"

"I mean it's all tied together. The predictions, the problems. I mean someone deliberately planned all these things. Someone is out to get us. Someone who knows about the fortune."

Leslie told Trisha about the frightening birthday phone call. On the other end of the line, Trisha fell silent. Finally she asked, "Who do you think this someone is?"

"I don't know," Leslie answered, considering. She didn't want to accuse anyone, to say anything out loud. "It could be anyone. A friend. An enemy. Maybe it's someone who has a grudge against us both."

Leslie fell silent, thinking about Deborah.

Deborah, feeling shut out of Leslie's life. Harboring secret resentments about Steve.

Then there was Steve himself, caught up in strong feelings for both cousins.

"Or," Leslie contined, "maybe it's someone who's only after me, but is using the prediction as some kind of cover."

Caroline, Leslie thought. Without a doubt, she falls into that category.

And Rick. Her boyfriend, seemingly so close to her, so concerned. Yet at times Leslie had the most curious sensation. A feeling she couldn't really name. Not quite distrust. Not quite doubt.

"But what about my haircut?" Trisha asked. "That was total bad luck."

"I don't know," Leslie admitted, still not willing to point the finger at Deborah.

"We have to think this over," Trisha told her. "Figure things out. But right now you need to get some sleep. Try and relax."

Leslie snorted. But she did feel a little better. Just sharing all this crazy stuff with Trisha made it easier to bear.

"Who knows," Trisha went on soothingly. "Maybe this is as far as it goes. Maybe nothing more will happen."

A few minutes later, Leslie hung up. Tired and drained, she decided to follow Trisha's advice. She'd go to sleep early. Things always seemed brighter in the morning.

She called good night to her parents as she got ready for bed. Then she crawled under her blanket, stretching out over the cool, comforting sheets.

Leslie wriggled her toes, feeling safer than she had in a long while. Trisha made good sense. Who knew if the craziness would even continue?

In no time at all Leslie was sleeping peacefully, dreaming of Rick, of being held tight and secure in his arms. They swayed to soft music. The perfect dancer, Rick spun her out, then pulled her back in. But instead of Rick, she came face to face with strangers. Rows and rows of them, wearing dark, heavy clothes, their heads bowed in sorrow. Leslie looked down at her simple black dress.

She was at a funeral.

Murky light filtered into the room. Baskets of flowers gave the air a sickly sweet smell. Leslie knelt to touch a silky leaf. The petals crumbled into dust, dirtying her hands.

Then she noticed the coffin. It stood at the front of the room, resting on the bare wooden floor. The lid yawned open.

Leslie couldn't see a body. She couldn't see much of anything. Only the big gaping coffin, luring her to peek inside. Pulling her closer.

Edging nearer, Leslie's heartbeat quickened. She wanted to turn back, to leave the room. Escape the funeral. But something drew her forward. Some morbid curiosity. Some force beyond her control. Her feet dragged her forward. Closer to the coffin.

A body jerked up suddenly. "Granny!" Leslie cried.

Slowly Granny Barrows pivoted her body so she faced Leslie. She wore the same green dress she'd worn to her eightieth birthday party, and her green eyes sparkled brightly. Deathly pale, she radiated energy. Her eyes drilled into Leslie's. She stared right at her. Right through her. Then she pointed one gnarled old finger.

"Be careful," Granny warned, her voice quavering. "Birthday parties can be deadly."

Her message delivered, she lifted her arm to grasp the coffin lid. Slowly, she began to close it. The hinges creaked. The wood groaned loudly.

Leslie heard it so clearly. She saw the cover

come down. She felt the coffin quilting beneath her head.

Powerless to move, she watched the wedge of light grow smaller, the darkness greater. Leslie shivered — with fright, with cold. The coffin lid banged down.

She was trapped inside!

It was so cold in the coffin, so very black and cold. She had to escape. She had to move. Pushing against the top, she gasped, her breath escaping in short sudden bursts.

The lid wouldn't budge.

Leslie shifted, bringing her shoulder against the heavy wooden lid. She pressed with all her strength, gathering up every ounce of force she could muster.

The lid popped open. She could breathe! With one quick leap, she scrambled out of the coffin . . .

. . . and hit her bedroom floor.

Her bedroom floor?

The coffin was really her bed, the lid only her blanket. She'd had a nightmare. Another horrible nightmare.

Soft morning light slanted through her bedroom curtains. Leslie checked her alarm clock. Six forty-four. Her alarm would go off in another minute. Leslie quickly turned it off before it sounded. The loud, jarring noise would be too much to take. Her nerves felt tight as a drum.

Moving as though she were still in a dream, Leslie showered and dressed. No makeup this morning, she decided. She felt too shaky to handle the small brushes and wands.

Leslie rubbed her swollen red eyes. Her head was in a fog, still fuzzy from the nightmare, from her fitful night's sleep. Breakfast didn't help clear her mind. Maybe a walk would do the trick.

Leslie called Rick. "I think I'm going to walk to school this morning," she told him when he answered.

Her tongue felt thick, like she had the flu, and she seemed to be speaking slowly. But Rick didn't notice. "So don't pick me up," she continued. "I can use the exercise and some fresh air."

"You're going to walk?" Rick sounded surprised — and annoyed. "I feel like we haven't spent any time together at all, Leslie."

He lowered his voice tenderly. Confidentially. "I can tell something's going on with you. Don't shut me out, Les. You need me."

"I'm fine," Leslie insisted, keeping her voice steady. "I'll see you later. I promise."

"When?" Rick pressed. "Tonight? It's Friday. We can do something special. Just you and me."

Leslie pictured the two of them alone. A romantic setting, maybe, where she'd feel totally relaxed. "Okay," she agreed.

They said good-bye on slightly better terms than when they'd begun their conversation. Leslie hung up, but immediately the phone started to ring.

"Rick?" Leslie snatched it up, thinking he'd forgotten to tell her something. Leslie heard the background music from a morning talk show come over the line, and she realized her mistake.

"Hi, Deb."

"Hey, how did you know it was me?" Deborah asked, surprised.

Leslie knew if she told her, she'd get a full-blown synopsis of that morning's topic. "Just a guess."

"Oh. Well, how are you getting to school? I thought maybe you'd like to drive with me this morning."

Leslie slipped into a pair of sneakers, and hurriedly tied the laces. "I would," she told Deborah. "But I've decided to walk. And I have to go now if I want to get to school on time."

"Good-bye then," Deborah said coldly. "Don't let me keep you."

Before Leslie could protest, Deborah hung up. Leslie sat for a moment, staring at the silent phone. She knew she'd been abrupt with Deborah — and maybe with Rick as well. Regret washed over her. She didn't like to hurt anyone, and that seemed to be all she was doing lately.

She reached for the phone, to call one of them back, to apologize and accept a ride. But then she stopped, her hand in midair. She needed this time to be alone. To think.

Leslie left her house, no apologies extended.

But walking down the quiet tree-lined streets a moment later, Leslie began to doubt her decision. She'd wanted to mull things over. Categorize the incidents into neat little boxes, so she could sort them through. Coolly. Rationally. Instead, her dreams and nightmares and everything that happened came back to haunt her with incredible force, breaking into her thoughts, making her relive them all over again.

Leslie could feel the cold darkness of her dreams encircling her, closing in. In the distance, she heard the strains of children shrieking "Happy birthday."

Was that in her nightmare? Was that real life? Everything seemed fuzzy. Images flashed through her brain. Bloodstained, ripped clothing. Granny Barrows collapsing. Mr. Corr handing her the history paper. A coffin slamming shut. Rick hugging her, saying he'd take care of her. Granny Barrows pointing a shaky warning finger.

Leslie crossed High Street, oblivious to the sounds around her. A sudden screech of tires jolted her into wakefulness. She heard an engine gun directly behind her.

Leslie froze. Every fiber in her being shouted, Move! Get out of the way! But, in her panic, she couldn't move. Couldn't budge.

She couldn't even turn around.

The tires squealed again. The engine roared. The smell of burning rubber filled the air. The car leaped forward.

Right at her.

Chapter 16

Leslie felt the car bear down on her. Felt the rush of wind and heat. "Ah!" she cried, whirling around. She threw herself to the sidewalk. The car missed her by inches.

She heard it bounce wildly onto the sidewalk, crashing into garbage cans just ahead of her.

Leslie kept her head down and twisted into a roll. She hit the pavement hard. Her knapsack dug into her back. Gravel pressed into her skin.

The car rolled to a stop.

Leslie cowered behind a garbage can, thinking, There's nowhere to go. Nowhere to run.

The car revved its engine. Suddenly it reversed, careening backward onto the street, then racing away full throttle.

In a daze, Leslie lifted her head. She saw a flash of red speed into the distance.

Red? she wondered. Did a red car try to knock her down? Or was it an accident?

Maybe someone's steering got out of whack, and she just happened to be in the wrong spot at the wrong time.

Stumbling to her feet, Leslie wiped the dirt from her jeans. One spot was torn, where she'd landed on her knees. Blood seeped through the material, but it wasn't too bad.

I guess I'll live, Leslie thought, trying to laugh the whole thing off. But it wasn't quite working. She blotted at the cut with a tissue from her knapsack.

There were only a few more blocks to school. Not knowing what else to do, Leslie trudged on, steadying herself as she went. She touched parked cars and trees for support, to hold herself together. She didn't want to go off the deep end, imagining a deliberate attempt on her life.

But was it?

By the time she reached the school parking lot, Leslie still didn't feel sure — about anything. People swarmed around her. Car doors slammed. Voices rose and faded. But Leslie felt as if she were invisible. As if she could scream for help at the top of her lungs and no one would hear.

"Leslie!"

So, people can see me after all, Leslie thought. Relief flooded her body. She turned happily, eager to make contact. Then she saw who was calling her.

Steve.

He elbowed his way through a crowd of freshmen. They parted easily, intimidated by his fierce gaze and heavy scowl.

"Leslie!" he called again, his voice demanding and loud. Leslie found herself backing away.

Don't be silly, she told herself. She planted her feet on the ground and forced herself to stay put. It's only Steve. There's nothing to be afraid of.

Steve closed in. Leslie held her ground. But she couldn't help but flinch when he reached out to her.

Gripping her arm, he said, "I've been looking for you, Leslie." He stared directly into her eyes, not noticing her ripped jeans or disheveled hair. "We need to talk. A lot's been going on. There are things that need to be discussed. Now."

A few feet away, something — no, someone — caught Leslie's eye. Deborah was gesturing at her wildly, mouthing something Leslie couldn't make out.

She's desperate for me to stop talking to

Steve, Leslie realized. She wants her shot with him. Her opportunity.

Leslie shook her head, trying to rein in her emotions. Her eyes stopped on two cars, and suddenly Deborah and Steve grew fuzzy. Steve's voice became an indistinct murmur, Deborah's wild waves muted.

Leslie's stomach lurched with fear. She felt her hands turn clammy. How could she not have realized it sooner?

Deborah's family station wagon was parked next to Steve's old Volkswagen.

And both were red.

Chapter 17

Leslie pushed away from Steve. She didn't want to see or talk to anyone, least of all him. She needed to get away. Away from her friends . . . her enemies . . . away from school.

Rushing through the parking lot, Leslie kept her head down. She'd go home. Skip classes. She'd never cut out before — never left school before walking through the doors. But this was an emergency. It called for extreme measures.

Leslie raced back up the streets she'd stumbled down minutes earlier. She wanted the safety of her home, the comfort of her own familiar bedroom.

Crazy plan after crazy plan flew through her mind as she pounded the sidewalk.

I'll hire private detectives to guard me, she thought. I'll sneak into Steve's car and check for clues. It won't be that difficult. He keeps a spare set of keys under the fender.

Then she quickly discarded that for another idea. I'll never leave the house. I'll stay there safe and protected and take correspondence courses to finish school.

No. I'll transfer to a boarding school in Switzerland.

Wait. I'll hide out in Sharon's dorm room.

Finally Leslie reached her front door, and paused to catch her breath. As her breathing slowed to normal, her thoughts slowed down, too.

Pretending she could run away was all well and good. But really, it was just a fantasy. She had to concentrate on real solutions. Real questions.

Whom could she trust? Whom should she stay away from?

Practically everyone, Leslie decided, until I know who's doing these things. Or until my party is over. The red cars didn't prove anything. Steve and Deborah were just two possibilities.

So what should she do about her date that night with Rick?

Inside her house, Leslie grabbed a diet Coke and retreated to her room. Flipping through the channels on TV, she thought things over.

How could she really suspect Rick, her boyfriend? Just yesterday, he'd stood up for her in front of all their friends when someone called her a cheater.

"What happened to innocent until proven guilty?" he'd scoffed. "Besides, I know Leslie would never cheat. And I'll take on anyone who says otherwise."

The girl had quickly backed down, and Leslie, eyes brimming with tears, had accepted her apology.

Rick would do anything to protect her. And even if he enjoyed playing the hero role, what was wrong with that?

Nothing, Leslie reasoned. In fact, what could be better, considering the danger she might be in?

Still, she couldn't quite convince herself. Nagging doubts kept tugging at her brain. Questions about Rick's relationship with Caroline . . . why she needed to hold on to him so desperately.

Was it just crazy Caroline, or did Rick manipulate her into needing him?

Hours passed while Leslie stared zombielike at the TV screen, not able to make up her mind. Morning turned to afternoon, and Leslie fell into a deep, dreamless sleep. She woke suddenly to the sound of a police siren on a news show. Her heart pounded loudly.

I've got to get hold of myself, she thought.

I'll take a walk. Get some fresh air. She left a note for her parents saying she had left school early because she wasn't feeling well, took a nap, and then felt better, so she went to the library.

She wandered around aimlessly, unaware of the darkening sky. By the time she got back, it was 6:15. Rick would be there any minute.

It was too late to call off the date.

I can still get out of it when he comes over, Leslie thought. Make some kind of excuse.

She bent over the kitchen sink, splashing water on her face. Yes, that was exactly what she'd do. She'd say she was tired. If Rick was really concerned — as concerned as he said he was — he'd surely understand.

On the refrigerator, Leslie found a note from her parents saying they were glad she felt better. They were at Aunt May's for the evening — she should call if she needed them. On Leslie's answering machine in her bedroom, there was also a slew of messages from Rick, asking where she was. Why wasn't she in school? Was everything all right?

Leslie sighed as she went back into the kitchen and halfheartedly searched through the cabinets for something to eat. She'd have to answer those questions when she saw him. And then she'd send him on his way.

Leslie was just opening a jar of peanut butter when Rick pulled into the driveway.

She gazed at him through the kitchen window. He threw open the convertible door and jogged across the driveway, his thick blond hair blowing in the wind. His body looked so strong and athletic, it seemed to glow.

Hurriedly, Leslie put away the peanut butter, then ran a hand through her hair. Maybe she'd go, after all.

"Hey, Les," Rick called, slipping gracefully through the back door. He leaned down to kiss her. His lips brushed hers so softly, so sweetly, Leslie melted against his chest.

"It's good to see you," she said, her voice catching. "I'm sorry I didn't call you back. I wasn't feeling well, so I left school early."

Rick lifted her chin so she looked into his eyes. "I'm glad to see you're better. Will you be okay tonight?"

"I think so."

"Good, I missed you. Now don't worry about a thing. I know you've had a lot on your mind, so I planned the entire evening."

Just like always, Leslie thought, pulling away slightly. But then Rick brought her to his car, and showed her a picnic basket in the back seat. The basket overflowed with fruit and bread and a generous portion of barbecued chicken. A delicate set of silver candlesticks rested against the seat, and a pretty flowered blanket was folded next to the basket.

"It's a beautiful night," Rick whispered in her ear. "And I know the prettiest spot. We can watch the sunset from the top of Mount Porter. I even brought my portable CD player and tons of CDs, perfect for a romantic picnic."

The air felt warm, with a sweet spring breeze, and Leslie imagined the gorgeous sun setting while she cuddled next to Rick. It was the kind of thing she used to dream about.

"It sounds wonderful," she said.

Briefly, she toyed with the idea of asking Rick if she could drive. She hadn't practiced in a while, and she definitely needed more experience on country roads. But she bit back the suggestion. She was still feeling antsy from that morning. And Rick would just say no, he liked driving. He liked Leslie's eyes on him, knowing he was responsible for her. He liked taking care of her. And Leslie didn't want to stir anything up. The night felt perfect so far, and she didn't want to spoil it. She was feeling too good, just being with Rick.

The feeling stayed with her through the long drive to Mount Porter. The top was down on the convertible, and a pretty, dusky light settled over town. Heading away from houses and stores, they soon rolled along empty country roads. They passed signs for steep inclines and sharp turns. Rick took each one expertly.

Leslie leaned her head against Rick's shoulder. She closed her eyes, feeling peaceful and secure as the car climbed uphill. Sheer drops bordered the car on either side. Flimsy guardrails stood etched in the gray light, like aging sentinels.

"We're almost there," Rick told her quietly. Leslie smiled, lulled by the motion of the car and the soft music.

A loud noise suddenly shattered the stillness. A sputtering sound filled the air. The car jerked once, twice, then slowed to a stop.

"What?" Rick said, surprised.

Leslie peered outside. They were just a few feet from the edge of the mountain. She leaned forward, her eyes wide open now. "What's wrong?" she asked.

"I'm not sure," Rick answered. "The car just conked out."

He turned the ignition key. The engine roared to life, choked, then died. Shaking his head, he tried it again. This time, he turned the wheel so the car slid to the shoulder of the road, inches from the guardrail. Then the engine fell silent.

Groaning, Rick turned the key again. The engine didn't even turn over.

Leslie didn't want to keep looking out at the mountain. She didn't want to notice the break in the guardrail, right where the car had stopped. Instead, she ran her eyes over the dashboard, looking for some sort of sign of what went wrong. The needle on the gas gauge pointed straight at empty. Her heart sank.

The scene was right out of an old movie. The guy making the moves on the girl, arranging ahead of time to stop on a deserted country road.

"Looks like I ran out of gas," Rick said, eyeing the gauge too. "Not a big deal. There's a gas station a little way back. I'll just run over and be right back with a gas can."

He leaped out of the car, before Leslie could say a thing. It barely registered that Rick didn't have designs on her after all. The idea of being alone was too terrifying.

"No!" She reached out to hold him back. "Don't leave."

Rick grinned, tenderly stroking her hand. "Don't worry. I've got everything under control. I'll be back before you know it." He tousled her hair. "All you have to do is wait."

With that, Rick turned on his heel and disappeared into the growing darkness. Leslie hugged her knees to her chest, suddenly cold. The night was still. The mountain was deserted.

And Leslie was stranded, all alone.

Grave trouble.

Chapter 18

The night grew darker. The sun had set, so quickly, it seemed, Leslie didn't even realize it. She'd thought she would witness all of nature's glorious colors. But no, she didn't even have that small comfort.

Leslie huddled against the seat as a chill wind sprang up, fanning her hair across her eyes. How much time had passed since Rick left? Leslie wasn't sure. Scared and cold, she wished the date would end. She wanted to be back home safe and sound, the entire day behind her.

Grave trouble.

Something could happen at any moment. Something terrible.

Leslie searched for a flashlight in the glove compartment. She needed some light, some reassurance. Luckily, her fingers closed around the smooth cylindrical shape. She drew it out, then quickly switched it on. Its dim bulb lit a small circle around her. But the tiny light only made the night seem darker.

An owl hooted. Leslie jumped in fright. How many other animals were out on the mountain roads roaming around? Just waiting for some poor desperate traveler to get stuck?

"That's enough," she said out loud. "At least I can try to get the top up on the convertible. That would give me some protection."

Immediately she felt better. Having a plan of action helped.

Edging carefully around the car, she felt her way to the back. She tugged on the top, and it sprang up easily. "All right!" she cried. Then it stopped, sticking straight up.

Leslie pushed and pulled, but the top wouldn't go up the rest of the way. Leslie had a sinking feeling that she needed to turn on the ignition. But part way was better than no way. She was lucky she'd moved it at all. And as Leslie scrambled back into the front seat, she felt a little more secure.

"Now!" she said, relieved that her voice sounded so steady. "I'll just turn on some music."

Leslie switched on the portable CD player. Soothing music filled the car, masking the sounds of the night. Leslie began to relax.

What could happen out here in the middle of nowhere? She hadn't told anyone where she was going. And if someone had followed, surely they'd already have made themselves known. They would have done something, frightened her somehow. Too much time had passed.

Her shoulders, tensed and stiff, loosened up.

Leslie hadn't thought it possible, but the night grew darker still. Even with the flashlight, Leslie could barely see two inches from her face.

Out of nowhere, something hurtled through the windshield. A rock. Right at her. In a flash, Leslie ducked below the glove compartment.

The sound of shattering glass ripped through the night. Shards pelted the front seat, aimed like arrows into the passenger seat. They tore into the fabric. They rained down on Leslie's feet.

The CD player smashed to bits. The music stopped.

Leslie held her breath, listening. It was quiet — deadly still — as if the world had ended.

Carefully, Leslie backed out of her little shelter. Glass crunched beneath her heels. With her back to the door, she felt for the handle. She wanted to get out of the car. Away from the edge of the mountain.

But suddenly, the car began to rock. Leslie heard the thud of someone pushing down on the trunk, then silence as the car bounced up.

She couldn't look out the back. The top blocked any view. But someone was definitely there, intent on nosing the car along — maybe pushing it through the guardrail opening . . . over the cliff!

A strangled cry escaped Leslie's lips. Should she try and get out of the car? Face her attacker? Or would she be safer inside, on the chance the car was too heavy to budge?

She was afraid to move; afraid any forward movement would send the car hurtling into nothingness. Seconds ticked by like hours. She felt herself grow hot with worry. Beads of sweat ran down her neck. The steady *thud thud* . . . the ominous rocking continued.

Finally, shouting with all her might, she half flipped, half flopped into the backseat. She felt the picnic basket collapse under her weight. Then she flung open the door and threw herself out — just as the rocking stopped.

Leslie crouched on the ground by the rear tire. The guardrail loomed in front of her. The car hadn't moved an inch.

Where was the attacker? Gone into the

darkness? Already on the main highway, heading into town?

Leslie shivered as another blast of cool air swept around the bend. She wiped her forehead with the back of her hand, her perspiration already drying. She felt frozen in place.

Then she heard a rustling noise.

Chapter 19

"Leslie?"

"Rick!" Leslie shouted. Released from her crouch, she threw herself into his arms. Before she could think, before she could wonder, she was hugging him tight.

"Whoa!" He laughed, holding the gas can over her head with one hand. His other hand gripped a flashlight and his arm circled her waist. "If I'd known I'd get this kind of reception, I'd leave you stranded more often."

Still clutching his hand, Leslie bent to find the flashlight she'd dropped. Then she waved it over the front seat, over the shattered windshield and broken glass.

"S-s-s-omething happened," she stuttered. "Somebody threw a rock at the windshield. And then, and then — " she could barely bring herself to tell him — "they rocked the car back and forth. Back and forth. I thought it was going over the cliff. With me in it!"

"I can't believe it!" Rick peered at the damage, shocked. He swept the broken bits of glass off the seat in one angry motion. Then he trained his high-powered flashlight around the empty windshield.

"Hey!" Leslie said, suddenly suspicious. "Where did you get that flashlight?"

Did he have it all along, leaving Leslie floundering with a flashlight that barely worked? Knowing she wouldn't be able to see her attacker?

"I got it at the gas station." Rick shook his head, confused. "Why?" Without waiting for an answer, he sat heavily behind the wheel. "This whole thing stinks! It was probably some dumb kid out joyriding, trying to scare you just for laughs."

He smacked the wheel. "And now I have to pay for all this damage." He turned to Leslie, who was still standing outside. Drawing her close, he murmured, "And poor you, stuck out here all alone. I'm so sorry I left you."

He led her around to the passenger side, and helped her inside. "You just sit here. I'll take care of everything."

Rick filled the gas tank, tossed the can in the trunk, and then cleared off the jagged glass from the windshield frame.

Leslie held her breath as he started the car, and let it out only when the engine purred as if nothing had happened. Rick adjusted the top, and then they were off.

Leslie sat close by Rick the whole drive home. And when she said good night, she held him tight. He asked if she still wanted to do something, get something to eat, but Leslie felt so drained, she only wanted to crawl into bed.

"You'd better have some dinner," Rick advised. He twisted his head to look at their picnic dinner, crushed and ruined. "I'll call you later to make sure you're okay."

Rick watched Leslie go inside. And only when she was safely inside did he drive away. Sighing, Leslie fell onto the comfy living-room couch. It was only 7:45. Hard to believe she had been gone only a couple of hours.

Stretching, Leslie sighed again. She thought about making that same old peanut butter and jelly sandwich. But even that seemed to require too much effort. She'd just lie here, read a magazine, maybe nap until her parents came home from Aunt May's. Leslie drifted off to sleep.

Suddenly, she awoke with a start.

Aunt May. Trisha! The realization hit Leslie like a thunderbolt.

If she'd been in danger earlier, Trisha could be in danger right this minute! She had to warn her!

Leaping from the couch, Leslie raced to the phone. She dialed the number and waited. The phone rang once. Twice. Three times. "Come on, pick up," Leslie moaned. "Someone answer."

The machine started up. "Hi!" Trisha said brightly in the recorded message. "We're not home right — "

"Hello! Hello!" a voice said breathlessly, cutting off the machine.

"Aunt May?"

"Leslie, is that you?"

"Yes. I have to talk to Trisha. It's important."

"Leslie." Aunt May took a deep breath, then continued. "Trisha's in the emergency room at the hospital. Your parents are already in the car waiting to take me there. We were just about to leave, but I rushed back to answer the phone. I thought it might be Trisha calling again."

Leslie stood still, praying she'd misunderstood, but knowing she hadn't.

"What happened?" she whispered.

"Someone pushed her down the stairs at the mall."

Chapter 20

Leslie's parents picked her up on the way to the hospital. They sped to the center of town, and ten minutes later dropped her and Aunt May off at the emergency room entrance.

The emergency room was empty, save for one nurse at the reception area and an old man holding a handkerchief up to his bleeding nose.

"My daughter," Aunt May said, gasping. "She's here."

"Patricia Barrows," Leslie added, leaning over the counter in her rush to find out Trisha's condition. "Is she okay?"

The nurse rose from her chair to check a file. "I'm not sure. I'll have to talk to the doctor and let you know. Please take a seat."

Leslie and Aunt May stayed right where they were while the nurse disappeared behind a swinging door. A few minutes later, she returned, smiling brightly. "She's doing fine.

Luckily, she escaped serious injury. She has a sprained ankle. And she's badly shaken up. But as I said, she's really doing fine."

Leslie collapsed against the counter, smiling back at the nurse. Aunt May grinned. "Can we see her?"

"Of course."

A minute later, Leslie hovered over Trisha in a curtained-off area, while Aunt May spoke to the doctor.

"Are you sure you're okay?" Leslie asked anxiously. Trisha lay in bed, her bandaged ankle propped over some pillows. Her face was white, drained of color. She looked exhausted.

Trisha nodded. "I'm okay." She grinned faintly. "At least that's what they tell me. I don't have to stay overnight or anything. I can go home."

Trisha faced Leslie, her face growing even paler. "I'm lucky. It could have been a lot worse."

What did Trisha mean, a lot worse? She could have had a broken leg? A broken collarbone? She could have plunged to her . . .

Leslie couldn't even think the word. "Did you see anything? Anybody?"

Trisha shook her head. "It all happened so quickly. I was in a crowd of people, going down the escalator. You know, the one by the big clock? There was some kind of commotion behind me. I heard somebody pushing — his way? Her way? I don't even know — down the stairs. Then I felt two hands on my back. They shoved — hard — and I just toppled. I managed to keep standing somehow until the very end . . . until I hit the floor . . . and that's when I tripped and twisted my ankle."

"Ouch!" Leslie said sympathetically.

"Then all these people rushed over to help, and whoever pushed me disappeared."

"Did anyone else see — " Leslie began, but Aunt May strode over, with Leslie's parents trailing behind.

"We're all set." Aunt May helped Trisha to her feet. Then she handed her a crutch. "We can go home now, sweetie."

"Please!" Leslie pleaded as an idea popped into her mind. "Can Trisha stay with me tonight?"

Aunt May looked uncertain. "Well, I don't know. I'd feel better if Trisha was in her own bed, at home."

Leslie didn't want to say, "Trisha and I both need company." That would make her parents suspicious. She exchanged glances with Trisha. "I'm fine, Mom," Trisha said. "And I'd really like to sleep over at Leslie's."

"Trisha can have my bed," Leslie offered quickly, "so she'll be comfortable. I'll take the cot."

Leslie's mother put her hand on Aunt May's arm. "We'll look after her, May. Why don't you come over for a while so we can all spend some time together?"

It was decided. Everyone went back to the Barrows' house. After a makeshift dinner, and frequent assurances that Trisha would be fine, Aunt May left. Not long afterward, the cousins settled into bed. Leslie swung her legs over the end of the cot while she twisted to look at Trisha in bed.

Finally, they'd be able to really talk things over. There were so many things they had to discuss. Quickly, Leslie told her about the incident at Mount Porter.

Trisha's eyes opened wide. "That's so scary!" she exclaimed. "At least I was at the mall with about a million people around."

"This is really getting dangerous." Leslie propped a pillow under her head and tried to get comfortable on the tiny cot. "I know we agreed to keep quiet about everything, Trisha. But it's so out of hand now. I'm frightened."

Trisha mumbled, "Me, too."

Leslie glanced over. Her cousin's eyes were

half-closed, and her head drooped to one side.

"What do you think we should do?" Leslie asked.

"Can we talk about it tomorrow?" Trisha's eyes shut the rest of the way, and she breathed heavily in and out. Seconds later, she began to snore.

Leslie sighed. Her mind raced with questions. How could she ever fall asleep? Surely she'd be up all night. But soon enough, Leslie felt her eyelids grow heavy, the events of the past few weeks taking their toll.

Leslie shifted from side to side on the narrow cot. Falling into a restless sleep, she began to dream.

Storm clouds were gathering overhead. The air felt hot, humid. The night seemed so strange, Leslie wasn't sure where she was. Then she realized: She was at home, on the night of Granny Barrows's eightieth birthday party.

A crowd of people suddenly materialized. Party guests. Deborah stood hunched in a corner, only she looked the way she did now. A little plump, wearing an oversized man's shirt.

"Did you catch *Oprah* today?" she was asking Mrs. Krashmer.

Leslie turned away, only to spy Caroline standing inches away. "Great party," she said with a sneer. "I haven't had this much fun since my tonsils came out."

Then Rick strolled over. Ignoring Leslie, he put his arm around Caroline and whispered to her softly. Leslie just watched, until Steve pushed his way through the crowd. "You and me," he hissed. "You and me." He pressed his fingers into her upper arm.

Leslie pulled away. What were all these people doing here? She spun around, searching for her parents.

Deborah, Caroline, Rick, and Steve faded away. But the other guests — the real ones, Leslie felt sure — pressed in close. At first she was relieved. They would protect her. They were Granny Barrows's friends. They loved her.

But then they stretched long, grasping arms to hug her. "So much like Sophie," they cooed. Their grins grew wide and grotesque, their features distorted as though they were prisoners in a funhouse mirror.

Backing away, Leslie edged into a corner.

"Hello, sweetheart." Granny Barrows suddenly stood before her. Her emerald ring sparkled in the light; her eyes gleamed with intensity.

"Granny!" Relief flooded through Leslie's body.

"Don't worry," Granny urged soothingly. "None of this is real. It's all just a warning. Just a caution."

The next instant, Granny collapsed on the floor. She grasped the hem of Leslie's dress, pulling her down . . . down . . . It was the stroke, happening all over again, and this time Granny was dying right before her eyes.

It didn't seem like a dream at all.

"Leslie!" Granny whispered. Leslie knelt beside her. She knew Granny was trying to tell her something. Something important.

"Be careful," Granny choked out. "See how tragedy strikes a birthday celebration?"

Suddenly everything went black — and cold. Icy walls closed in. She could feel them pushing against her, pressing in tight. Leslie shivered in the suffocating darkness, in the frigid midnight blackness. She was so cold, so scared, she couldn't breathe. But she had to shout. She had to cry out.

Chapter 21

Leslie woke up, screaming. She rocketed out of bed. Her head snapped back and she gasped, clutching her blanket with both hands. Trembling, she blinked in the early morning light.

"Les? Are you okay?" Trisha flipped to her side, gently shifting her twisted ankle, to check on Leslie.

Leslie didn't answer. She soaked up every detail of her room. The pictures in the mirror. The soft quilt on her bed.

The sun streamed through lace curtains at the window. A blue jay hopped on the sill, twittering softly. Yes, she was in her bedroom. Not at her grandmother's party, not in some close dark place where the very air strangled her.

But Leslie didn't quite believe it. The dream

felt too real. Too frightening. Her knees felt weak. Her head pounded.

Was she all right, Trisha asked. She hadn't been all right for weeks. Burying her head in her hands, she told Trisha, "I had a nightmare."

The bedroom door burst open. Leslie's mother rushed in, tying her robe. "What happened? I heard screaming."

Trisha caught Leslie's eye, shaking her head to keep quiet. Smiling weakly, Leslie turned to her mother. "I'm fine. We're both fine. I just had a bad dream. That's all." Leslie tried to keep her voice light.

Relieved, Mrs. Barrows went downstairs to make breakfast. But as soon as she left, Leslie crumpled, falling back into bed. All her fears, all her worries poured out, rushing from her lips like water from a spout.

"I can't take this anymore," she whispered fiercely. "I'm afraid I'm going to wind up dead. I'm afraid we'll both wind up dead. I want to tell my parents everything. I want to tell the police, too. And you know what, Trisha? I want to call this whole stupid party off. Maybe that will stop the trouble. If we don't celebrate, if we don't even recognize our birthdays, maybe it will stop. Because . . ."

Leslie moved to the bed, sitting close to

Trisha for comfort. "Because whoever is doing this is serious. Dead serious."

Wincing, Trisha propped a pillow under her bad ankle. Then she took Leslie's hand, and gazed at her earnestly. "I know how serious this is," she said pointedly. "But my mom is worried enough, what with the divorce and all the money problems. I know if you call your Sweet Sixteen off, there's no way she'll say yes to mine. And I really really want one, Les."

Trisha paused for a moment, with downcast eyes. "I feel like it'll be a turnaround for me or something. I'll have a fun great party, and then things will start getting better. I won't feel so alone."

Leslie rubbed her eyes, her headache getting worse by the minute. "Of course you want a Sweet Sixteen. I want one, too. But who knows what could happen to us?"

"I don't think anything will," Trisha said firmly. "No one's about to kill us, Leslie. You're just being superstitious. That's the way you've always been, and now you're convinced the 'grave' in grave trouble means something serious. Besides," she added, lowering her voice. "If you really believe this prediction, you believe it will come true. No matter what."

Leslie gazed out the window, thinking. A cool breeze ruffled the curtains. The air smelled sweet. Clean. The sun slanted into the room, lighting the picture of Rick and making everything seem safe.

Really, Leslie reasoned, who could believe in predictions and an old woman seeing the future, on a perfect spring morning?

Trisha was right. She was always the first to fall for anything related to fate or superstitions. But they were talking about her life. Hers, not some character in a book, destined to die by the last chapter. And bad things didn't happen in her life, not really. There had to be a happy ending.

Besides, how would she explain her sudden decision to cancel her party? It would seem too ridiculous for words.

"Okay." Leslie smiled. Then she added, joking, "I'll be the guinea pig here. If I survive my Sweet Sixteen, you can go ahead with yours."

Leslie straightened her shoulders. The decision was made. She'd have her party.

Even if it killed her.

PART FOUR

May 11, 1996

Chapter 22

Two days later, Leslie woke to the radio's weather report: extremely muggy. Thunderstorms. Record highs for May, perhaps exceeding the highest temperature ever, recorded on May 8 three years ago.

May 8? The day of Granny's stroke.

Leslie hadn't been able to sleep all night. Torn between excitement and dread about the party, she'd stayed in a kind of sleepy wakefulness . . . a limbo . . . for hours on end. She'd been relieved when the alarm finally went off.

But now, Leslie wished she could roll over and block everything out. She didn't want a day like three years ago. She didn't want record high temperatures, storm clouds, and thunder.

Already, Leslie felt the heaviness in the air. She tossed off her blanket and swung her legs off the bed. "So what?" she told herself. "So what if it's hazy, hot, and humid? There's lots of days like this all spring and summer. It doesn't mean a thing."

Leslie turned off the radio, not wanting to hear any more bad news. The last couple of days had been a flurry of activity, taking care of last-minute details for the party, making final arrangements. Nothing else had happened — no other mishaps — and Leslie had begun to look forward to the celebration once again. She'd managed to squash her fears. Until now, when the whole nightmare came crashing back.

"Leslie, are you up?" her mother called from downstairs. "Your father and I have something special to give you."

"I'll be right down." Slipping on her robe, Leslie padded down the steps and into the kitchen. Her father smiled when he saw her.

"It's the Sweet Sixteen girl!" he said, putting down his newspaper. "Are you all set for the big day?"

Leslie gave a feeble grin. The newspaper headline glared up at her: SCORCHER TODAY! DOCTORS SAY BE CAREFUL — HEALTH RISKS POSSIBLE.

Great, thought Leslie, sinking into a kitchen chair. Even the papers are predicting trouble.

"Hi, hon." Leslie's mother came into the kitchen carrying an ornate jewelry box. Its shiny dark wood had a deep rosy glow, and complicated designs were carved into its sides. Leslie recognized it immediately.

"That's Granny's," she said, surprised.

Her mother nodded. She sat next to Leslie, then took her hand. "Your grandmother wanted you to have this," she explained, "for your sixteenth birthday. She willed you her jewelry."

"Happy birthday, sweetheart," her father added. "Your grandmother always felt so close to you. I guess she wanted to be near you on this special day."

Leslie drew the jewelry box closer. She could scarcely believe all those beautiful bracelets, necklaces, and rings belonged to her. Slowly, she lifted the lid. And there, right on top, nestled into a velvety case, was Granny's emerald ring. The one she'd worn practically every day of her life.

"Go on," her mom urged. "Try it on."

Leslie hesitated. It seemed strange to wear her grandmother's ring, something she'd seen only on Granny Barrows's hand, nowhere else. It belonged to her grandmother — to no one else. But the ring had a warmth to it. A pull that Leslie couldn't resist. Finally slipping it on her ring finger, she felt a closeness with Granny Barrows. Their bond grew tighter. It seemed that she could draw on her grandmother's strength . . . on the resolve that helped her settle in a foreign land and make a success of her new life.

Leslie held her hand up to the light, examining the ring in the hazy morning sunshine. "It's so beautiful." She sighed, letting out her breath.

An answering cool breeze swept the hot, humid kitchen. Leslie felt a flutter of excitement in her stomach. Maybe everything would work out fine after all.

"And do you know what?" she told her parents. "I'm ready for my Sweet Sixteen."

The lights dimmed. A streak of lightning split the sky, and a roar of thunder crashed over the house. The storm had begun.

Chapter 23

"It feels so good to be in a nice air-conditioned place."

"Have you tried the yogurt drinks in the concession stand? They're delicious."

"Ice skating when it's ninety-three degrees out. I love it."

"Yeah. What a cool idea for a Sweet Sixteen."

"Hey! Watch me go backward."

Leslie slowly skated around the rink, listening in on people's conversations, moving to the piped-in music. Her skirt twirled out around her, then flitted back as soft as a butterfly. The party seemed to be a success. Everyone marveled at the idea of ice skating when it was hot enough to fry an egg on a sidewalk. The early morning storm had quieted, then died away. Leslie began to think the strange, humid weather added a festive note to the party. Even Deborah, taking small jerky steps on the ice, was talking to a few other kids. Caroline was in attendance, of course. But she steered clear of Leslie, and Leslie could almost pretend she wasn't there.

Rick swooped over just then, tucking his arm through hers. They skated cozily together through a few songs. Leslie kept her mind on how handsome he looked. How great it felt to be close to him. Certainly not on any prediction.

"I'm going to grab some popcorn," Rick told her, easing her close to the railing. "Want some?"

"No thanks. I think I'll talk to Sharon for a while."

Leslie glided over to her sister, who was resting a few feet away. "So far, so good," she said, crossing her fingers.

Sharon grinned. "Better than good. Everyone's having a great time. And look." She pointed to a sign against the near wall. "The rink is closing for repairs tomorrow. You're lucky you're having this extravaganza now."

Lucky. Maybe she *was* lucky. Leslie nodded as Trisha hobbled over on one crutch, bumping along the rubbery floor. Blades had sent her another tuxedo outfit, and even though she wouldn't be skating, Trisha had dressed for the event.

"Things are going great," she said, waving her crutch at the crowd of guests. "See? Aren't you glad you went through with this?"

"Went through with it?" Sharon turned to Leslie, surprised. "What does that mean?"

"Nothing," Leslie said quickly. "I was just having preparty jitters."

Across the rink, Rick gestured for her to come over. Saying good-bye to Trisha and Sharon, Leslie pushed off from the railing.

Leslie went round the long way, slowly sailing past Deborah. "So Sally Jessy had all these ex-best friends on the show," she was explaining to Donna's boyfriend, a fierce, angry look on her face. "And they all had one thing on their minds."

"Getting even."

How could she have thought Deborah was having a good time? Leslie's head suddenly began to pulse with tension. Her temples throbbed in time to the rock music blasting over the sound system. The unsettled feeling, the sensation that everything slanted a little off-center, hit her with heavy force. Leslie faltered, and groped for the rail to hold herself steady.

Getting even.

Pausing, she realized that Caroline stood a few feet away, talking softly to Donna. Caroline's words hung in the air, then washed over Leslie like a tidal wave. "Rick doesn't know it yet. But he's going to come crawling back to me. He doesn't realize he needs me, that's all. But he will. I swear to you, Donna. He will very soon."

Leslie forced herself to skate away. Would Rick need Caroline to console him . . . to listen sympathetically . . . to step in and replace his girlfriend after she . . .

"Leslie!"

Leslie skidded to a stop when she heard Steve shout her name.

"Leslie!" he repeated, shoving his face close to Rick's. He wasn't shouting to her at all. He was shouting about her. "You treat her like a china doll. But you can't protect her from everything."

Steve's eyes were red, as if he'd been up all night. His chin jutted out angrily, and he seemed ready to throttle Rick.

"You don't know a thing," Rick shot back. "But how could you? You'd better stay away from Leslie. I'm warning you."

Leslie rubbed her eyes. Everything . . . everybody . . . sounded so ominous. But what did it mean? They couldn't all be plotting against her. They couldn't all be ready to strike.

Her fears were getting the best of her. Her nerves frayed beyond comprehension.

Rick rocketed away, leaving Steve alone in the corner. I'll talk to Steve, Leslie thought, skating closer. Settle him down. Make him calm, somehow.

"Hey. This is a party," she said, keeping her tone light and playful. "My party. Don't you know it's bad form to argue with the hostess's boyfriend?"

Steve forced his lips into a smile. "Sorry. It's just that that guy gets me so mad."

He looked so vulnerable and defenseless, Leslie touched his shoulder. How could she think he would do anything to harm her? They'd known each other so long.

"I know you're on edge," she told him in a low voice. "I know how Trisha hurt you."

A strange expression came over Steve's face. Leslie hesitated, unsure if she should go on. But she had to. She had to clear the air.

"Trisha told me all about it," she plowed on. "How much she hurt you. And maybe I've hurt you, too. But — "

"Excuse me, Leslie. Steve." Aunt May hovered on the floor outside the rink. "But I just wanted to say good-bye. Trisha and I are going home to change and then head on to Flamingo's." She bent over the rail to peck Leslie on the cheek. "We'll see you later."

"Thanks, Aunt May." Leslie hugged her briefly, then turned back to Steve. He was gone.

And suddenly, friends and relatives swooped down on her from all sides to thank her for the skating party. The rink emptied out quickly. The staff was packing up equipment and clearing the ice. A few people milled around, gathering their things.

The first part of the party is over, Leslie thought, and nothing's happened. No matter what I thought, or how afraid I felt. I'm safe. Everything is fine. She did a quick pirouette in the rink, a sense of peace coming over her.

"I'm just going into the locker room to change," she called to her parents. Then she hurried into the small room in the back, not wanting to be the last one to show up at her own formal dinner. Already everyone had come and gone, leaving the locker room deserted.

Humming happily, Leslie sat down on a bench. Her dress hung in the floor-to-ceiling locker behind her. Not too much longer now, and she'd be wearing it. Showing off the gentle folds of the smooth, deep velvet. She'd be wrapped in Rick's arms, moving close to him on the dance floor. Happy. Content. That's what she'd be.

"Fortune-tellers? Predictions? Ha!" she said out loud, reaching down to unlace her skates. She slipped them off, and wriggled her toes. "I'm going to be just fine."

An instant later, she heard a click. The sound of a light switch being turned off. And Leslie was plunged into darkness.

Chapter 24

Leslie jerked up her head. Her heart did a flip-flop of surprise. Her mouth opened, but no sound came out.

"Hey!" she finally sputtered. Then she raised her voice. "Hey! Who turned off the lights?"

There was no answer. The room was still. Only Leslie's heavy breathing broke the silence.

She stood up, careful not to bang against the bench. The light switch must be around. Somewhere. If not the light switch, she'd find the door. She just had to get out of there. Now.

Inching along the wall lined with lockers, Leslie groped in the darkness. The room felt enormous, as if it stretched forever. Finally she touched the smoothness of heavy wood, then a knob. She had reached the door.

Her hand closed around the doorknob. Breathing easier, she turned it to the right, then to the left. The knob stayed in place, not turning an inch. She pushed against the door. Then she pulled. It didn't budge.

"This can't be happening," Leslie muttered, trying again and again. But it was.

The door was locked — and she couldn't open it.

Blackness engulfed Leslie from head to toe, and suddenly she felt dizzy with fear.

"Help!" she cried, panic raising her voice high. "Mom! Dad! I'm stuck in the locker room."

She listened for their footsteps, for their concerned voices calling to her. Again, there was silence.

She pounded on the door, her cries turning to hiccups.

Was she the only person in the building? Did the staff finish closing up? Had her parents left, thinking she'd somehow gotten another ride?

Leslie screamed again and again, but it did no good.

Unbidden, her nightmares rose before her. Those terrifying dreams of smothering in a dark, enclosed place. Of air pressing down on her, heavy black air. They seemed more real than ever. More real than the skating party that just ended. More real than her formal dinner minutes away.

Was this going to be it? The end? Her birthday prediction coming true at an ice rink?

A blast of cold air swirled around her. Leslie shivered with cold — with a sudden jolt of recognition. Her nightmare again! The part where she couldn't stop shaking . . . when her breath came out like puffs of smoke in the cramped, freezing — what was it? A coffin? A closet?

A floorboard creaked a few feet away. Leslie wheeled around. Somebody was there. She wasn't alone.

"Help!" she screamed, her fear rising in her throat. She swallowed it back down. She bit her lip, listening . . . straining to hear something — anything.

Tap, tap, tap.

A soft thumping sound, a rapping noise like something striking the floor, echoed close by. The sound of footsteps. Someone coming nearer.

"Who's there?" Leslie called, her voice quavering. "Please, who's there?"

No answer. Just the steady tap, tap, tap, coming nearer.

A picture of Granny Barrows flashed before

her, warning, pointing, like she'd appeared in her dream.

A whimper escaped Leslie's lips. Then she clamped her mouth shut tight. She knew this person . . . he, she, whoever it was . . . had been responsible for all those incidents. All those accidents. And it would all come down to right now. Right here in the locker room.

Stepping quietly, Leslie edged back to her ice skates. She reached down. Then she picked one up, holding it blade forward.

Tap, tap.

Leslie stood still as a statue. She struggled to make out where the noise came from. Which direction.

A thump, a sound of something being dropped, sounded behind her. She started to wheel around, to bring the blade up higher. But before she could defend herself, two strong hands pushed at her back. Leslie floundered, caught off balance. She tried to right herself. To fight back. But she was shoved — hard — into an open locker.

The door slammed behind her. A click, and it was locked.

Leslie squeezed her body around in the narrow space. She faced the front. Beating on the door, she cried out again and again. Then she stopped, listening. The door rang softly with the vibrations. Leslie heard that . . . and the same tap tap . . . the same footsteps moving across the room.

There was a click of a key turning a lock . . . a crack of light. Then the only sound Leslie heard was the beating of her heart.

She slumped against the door, the cool metal hitting her forehead.

"Help me! Someone, please!" she shouted, knowing no one was there.

What could she do to escape? Would she spend the whole night here, missing her party, missing her own Sweet Sixteen? Waiting in vain for rescue until the following morning, when the rink staff came on duty?

"No," she groaned, as a sudden realization hit. "No!" As of right now, the rink was closed for renovations. Nobody would be coming in the morning. Nobody at all.

Leslie wrapped her arms around herself for warmth. She shivered in the growing cold.

It is growing colder! Leslie thought, her heart racing. And even as she wondered if she were imagining things, she felt another drop in temperature. She felt the heavy moisture of her breath hanging in the locker.

The thermostat must have been tampered with! And the rink was closed. It would just get colder and colder, the temperature dropping who knew how low.

How long would it take her parents to call a search for her? To guess that she might, just might, be stuffed inside a tiny, cramped locker freezing to death in an ice-skating rink?

The darkness pinched in close, claustrophobic, frightening. It was just like her nightmares. Her worst dream coming true. Who could have done this to her? Who would want her out of the way this badly?

Something nagged at the back of her mind. Something about Steve's expression when she spoke to him before . . . something about those footsteps.

Leslie racked her brain. But it didn't help. She was feeling faint, drained of all energy, all hope of escape.

She felt as if she were spinning, falling through space.

The blackness closed in like a coffin lid banging shut.

Chapter 25

Slowly the spinning stopped . . . winding down like a child's top that totters, then falls. Leslie's stomach lurched, then settled. Her body drooped against the freezing metal locker door.

Leslie opened her eyes, not sure if she was dreaming. For there — right in front of her, as if the locker had no door, no sides — stood her grandmother, bathed in bright glowing light. Beckoning silently.

What did Granny want?

She wants me to come closer, Leslie thought, desperate to understand. She's trying to warn me. No! She's trying to tell me something important. How to escape.

That I *can* escape!

Leslie jolted into wakefulness. Her hand dug into something sharp. A blade of some sort. Her ice skate!

"My way out!" Leslie gasped.

Quickly, she wedged the blade into a crack in the locker door. Heaving all her weight against the skate, she felt the door give a bit, then snap back into place.

This had to work!

Again she pressed against the skate, this time from another angle. She leaned hard into the push, prying open the metal door so slowly, she thought it hardly budged at all. But the metal was bending a little at a time. Leslie pressed harder still, and suddenly the locker jerked open.

Leslie fell on the floor, landing on her knees, the room still shrouded in darkness.

She panted from the effort. Her shoulders heaved as she caught her breath. She took in great gasps of air, feeling the solid ground beneath her.

The tapping sound came back to her. And suddenly it hit her. The person responsible for every little thing that had happened — from the missing invitations to leaving her to die in a freezing locker.

A surge of energy brought Leslie to her feet. Fumbling in the dark, she scooped up her sneakers, then found her way to the door. Streetlights filtered through the windows, dimly lighting the rink. Leslie dashed for the exit.

Outside, dusk was turning into night. Leslie crouched, putting on her sneakers as quickly as she could. Then, still wearing her skating outfit, she raced down the street to Flamingo's.

She skirted the cars parked outside the restaurant, barely giving them a glance. Steve's Volkswagen, Deborah's station wagon. The convertible. Not pausing for a second, she burst through the entrance.

"What?" said the maitre d', staring at Leslie's skating outfit and sneakers.

Leslie brushed past him into the dining area. Inside, everyone was grouped in a circle, heads bent anxiously toward someone crying. Leslie heard the sniffles. The sound of someone trying to speak.

A Happy Birthday banner hung on one wall. A tall white cake — tiered like a wedding cake, but decorated with candles — stood on a separate table. Next to it, presents were piled up like a small mountain.

Not saying a word, Leslie pressed quietly against the far wall. This was it. The moment of truth. Whoever sat at the center of the circle would attempt to explain what happened. Why

Leslie wasn't at her own Sweet Sixteen dinner.

Then Leslie heard the voice. That old familiar voice. Smiling grimly, Leslie crossed her arms. She was right.

The person in the center was Trisha.

Chapter 26

"I know I should have told someone," Trisha wailed. She turned to Leslie's mother, a pleading look in her eyes. "I should have told you about the prediction . . . and . . . and everything! But Leslie told me to keep quiet. She convinced me. She said she didn't want you to cancel her party."

Trisha gulped, making her eyes big and frightened. "Then I saw her being shoved into a car by two big goons. I didn't recognize them. I couldn't tell you who they were. But they took Leslie!"

Moaning, Trisha rocked back and forth. "She could be dead by now, for all we know! She could be anywhere! And it's all my fault!"

"Yes," Leslie said quietly, stepping forward. "It is all your fault."

Trisha's head snapped up. Her eyes blazed at Leslie. "What? You're here? How?"

"Oh, Leslie!" Her parents rushed at her, engulfing her in big hugs. "We were so worried!" her mother cried, almost babbling with relief.

"We looked for you at the rink, then thought you'd found a ride with a friend. We weren't even concerned when you didn't show up right away. You know how you're always late! What did those men do to you?"

Leslie drew back. Everyone stared at her. Rick. Deborah. Caroline. Steve. They crowded closer, waiting for an explanation. And Leslie was ready to give it.

"There were no men. It was Trisha."

Her Aunt May turned red. "You're talking nonsense, Leslie. You're just overwrought."

Leslie ignored her, ignored everyone. She inched closer to Trisha, and talked directly to her cousin. "I figured it out after I heard the tapping sound in the locker room. It was your crutch hitting the floor. Everything — all your little accidents — were just tricks. Ploys to make me think someone was after you, too. You drained the gas from Rick's car, then rocked it on the mountain. You took the keys to Steve's car and tried to run me down."

Leslie's voice caught with emotion. "But why, Trisha? Why?"

Trisha opened her mouth, about to answer.

Then she leaped at Leslie, snarling. Steve jumped up, pinning her arms to her sides.

Everyone else stood frozen in place like exhibits in a museum. "Trisha," her mother choked out, still not able to move. "You don't know what you're doing."

Trisha glared at her mother. A deep red color suffused her face. Then she turned her anger back to Leslie.

"You've always had it so easy," Trisha spat out. "Everyone loved you, without you even trying. Your parents would never divorce. Oh no. Not Little Miss Perfect's. You'd never have money troubles . . . or any troubles, if it wasn't for me."

Then it all came tumbling out . . . how Trisha had been jealous of Leslie — especially her closeness with Granny Barrows. How, years ago, she'd overheard Granny talking to Leslie at her party. She'd known Granny had promised Leslie the emerald ring — the one piece of jewelry Trisha had always loved.

Suddenly Trisha crumpled to the floor, breaking free of Steve's hold. She started to sob. Real sobs, that racked her entire body.

"I just wanted to scare you," she cried. "I wanted you to cancel the party. Maybe even refuse the gifts. So I pretended to lose my earrings. I jumped up during my haircut so a whole chunk of hair got cut off. But then I had to keep it up. I had to make each one worse and worse. And then . . . after all that . . . when I couldn't even hold on to Steve . . . when I knew I'd lost him and had to do something, I wanted to hurt you. I didn't want you to cancel the party. I wanted revenge.

"I'm sorry," she choked out. "I am. Really, I am."

"Trisha." Tears ran down Leslie's cheeks now, too, streaking her makeup. She bent closer to Trisha, pain, anger, and sympathy tearing her apart.

"Get away!" Trisha reared up like a hissing snake. Her face contorted with fury.

Aunt May stepped forward. "Trisha, calm down," she said in a soothing voice. "Everything will be okay. We'll take care of everything."

"Just like you took care of your marriage?" Trisha whirled around to face her. "Just like you took care of your life?"

Leslie buried her head in her mother's arms, as Trisha advanced on Aunt May. "It's over," she shrieked wildly. "Everything is over. Can't you understand that?"

She stumbled to the other side of the room.

With one sweep of her arms, the gifts flew off the table, scattering onto the floor. "That's what I think of all of you!"

Leslie's father rushed to stop her. But Trisha lunged for the long, sharp cake knife lying on the table. "Stay back," she ordered. "Keep away."

Mr. Barrows halted, unsure what to do. Leslie stepped forward, her expression calm, her step steady. Whatever happened, it would be between her and Trisha. No one else. "Stay back, everyone," she ordered.

"Ha!" Trisha waved the blade toward Leslie. Then she grabbed hold of a lighter, near some extra candles. "It's my favorite cousin's Sweet Sixteen," she cried, a crazed gleam in her eyes. "And it's time to light the cake."

Leslie sprang forward. But in the blink of an eye, Trisha had lit the long, tapering candles.

Trisha laughed maniacally, a long, low growl that started deep in her throat. "Everyone! Celebrate! Blow out the candles!"

She flung the cake at Leslie. Leslie ducked. She heard a hiss, smelled her burning hair. The flaming cake grazed her head. Then it sailed into the air, hitting a wall of curtains.

Instantly the curtains billowed out, lighting up like a huge raging torch. A crackling sound filled the air as hot, licking flames spread from wall to ceiling. The fire blazed with the strength of the sun. An intense heat filled every corner.

Sprinklers poured water from the ceiling. But the fire seethed on. "Get out of here!" Mr. Barrows shouted. "Everyone!"

People crowded toward the door, choking and rubbing their eyes. But Leslie felt too tired to move. Her feet were like blocks of cement.

One by one her beautifully wrapped gifts caught on fire. The tables — with all the pretty tablecloths and flowers — crumbled to ashes. Her party was going up in smoke.

"Come on, Leslie!" Her mother grabbed her arm and dragged her outside.

Where was Trisha? Leslie craned her neck and saw Aunt May herding her toward the back door. In the distance, she heard the wail of fire engines' sirens.

Outside, people looked dazed as they wandered around the parking lot. Leslie dropped onto the curb. Then she sat, chin in hand, watching Flamingo's burn.

Silently, she gazed at the destruction. The wreckage of her sixteenth birthday. Yes, she realized, the prediction really did come true. A police car roared into the lot.

"My trouble is over," she whispered. "But Trisha's is only just beginning."

PART IV

August 27, 1996

Chapter 27

The sun glazed down, warming the top of Leslie's head. It felt healing, comforting. Not like the sticky oppressiveness of those humid days in May. In fact, most of the summer had been sunny and cool, the weather breaking right after Leslie's Sweet Sixteen.

Leslie sighed, putting on her sunglasses. She was standing at the foot of her grandmother's grave in the Medvale Cemetery, gazing at the engraved tombstone: BELOVED WIFE, MOTHER, AND GRANDMOTHER.

Stepping gingerly, she walked closer to the stone. Then she gently placed the flowers she'd brought in its shadow. "Thanks, Granny," she said softly.

Leslie sat back on her heels, surveying the pretty rolling hills of the cemetery. She hoped, somehow, her grandmother had heard and understood.

For a few moments longer Leslie rested, thinking back over everything that had happened, and the role her grandmother had played.

It's strange how things worked out, Leslie thought, slowly getting to her feet. The sun dipped behind a cloud. Leslie took off her glasses as she made her way out of the cemetery.

Strange and sad.

A week after her Sweet Sixteen, Leslie had broken up with Rick. It had been a difficult decision. But she knew that Steve was right. Rick did treat her like a fragile little doll, not a person. And it just didn't seem worth it. Leslie wanted to be a real person. An equal. She wanted to be a partner in a relationship, not a damsel in distress shut up in a tower.

Thinking about Rick, Leslie felt a surprising heaviness. For all her talk of love being a two-way street, she missed him. She missed seeing him early in the morning on the way to school. She missed talking to him late at night when it felt like they were the only two people still awake.

Leslie shook her head, clearing up the jumble of thoughts. She'd had a choice. She'd made it.

Relationships were funny things, she'd discovered. Whoever thought Deborah and Steve would wind up together? That's what Steve had wanted to discuss with her all along — his interest in her best friend.

Sure, Trisha had "officially" broken up with him. But that was because he'd been trying to break up with *her*.

And those long, searching looks, those impassioned pleas to talk things over? Steve had only wanted to clear everything with Leslie first. "Because," he'd told her weeks after the party, "after all is said and done, I still care about you. I still want to be friends."

When Leslie thought about Deborah and Steve, a giddy feeling came over her — a feeling that anything was possible.

As for Trisha, Leslie felt hopeful. She was getting round-the-clock care and counseling at a nearby hospital. Leslie hadn't been to visit her yet. The doctors claimed it might cause a setback in her recovery. But Aunt May, pulling herself together in another surprising development, had been unbelievably strong. She visited Trisha every day, giving her support and a ready ear.

"She's going to come out of this," she'd repeatedly told Leslie. "And she's going to need all the friends she can get."

Leslie had nodded, not even angry anymore.

Just sad. It seemed things were settling down, falling into some sort of routine. The nightmare was over.

A car horn beeped, breaking into Leslie's thoughts. She glanced up, surprised to find herself blocks from the cemetery. Then she saw Rick steer his black convertible up to the curb beside her.

"Need a lift?" he called.

"No thanks," she answered, her heart doing that same old flip-flop. "I can walk just fine."

But already Rick was jumping out to open the door for her. Hasn't he learned anything? Leslie wondered.

"What if you do the driving?" he asked teasingly.

Leslie blinked, and realized Rick held open the driver's-side door, not the passenger's.

"And afterward," he added, "you can treat me to lunch. Anywhere you choose."

"Anywhere?" Leslie said with a grin.

"Anywhere."

Maybe, Leslie thought, Rick had learned something after all. And maybe, just maybe, things weren't settled quite yet.

Will anyone live to be crowned?

HOMECOMING QUEEN

John Hall

Westdale High is celebrating its first homecoming in twenty-five years. And Melissa is so excited — she's nominated for homecoming queen! Then mysterious accidents start to happen — Melissa is nearly crushed by a huge sandbag and another candidate is attacked by a swarm of bees! *Someone* doesn't want Westdale High to crown a homecoming queen....

Reigning soon at a bookstore near you.

THRILLERS

D.E. Athkins

☐ MC45246-0 Mirror, Mirror $3.50

A. Bates

☐ MC45829-9 The Dead Game $3.99
☐ MC43291-5 Final Exam $3.50
☐ MC44582-0 Mother's Helper $3.99
☐ MC44238-4 Party Line $3.99

Caroline B. Cooney

☐ MC44316-X The Cheerleader $3.50
☐ MC43806-9 The Fog $3.50
☐ MC45681-4 Freeze Tag $3.99
☐ MC45402-1 The Perfume $3.50
☐ MC44884-6 The Return of
the Vampire $3.50
☐ MC41640-5 The Snow $2.75
☐ MC45680-6 The Stranger $3.50
☐ MC45682-2 The Vampire's
Promise $3.50

Richie Tankersley Cusick

☐ MC43115-3 April Fools $3.50

☐ MC43203-6 The Lifeguard $3.50
☐ MC43114-5 Teacher's Pet $3.50
☐ MC44235-X Trick or Treat $3.50

Carol Ellis

☐ MC44768-8 My Secret Admirer .$3.50
☐ MC44916-8 The Window $3.50

Lael Littke

☐ MC44237-6 Prom Dress $3.50

Christopher Pike

☐ MC43014-9 Slumber Party $3.50
☐ MC44256-2 Weekend $3.99

Edited by T. Pines

☐ MC45256-8 Thirteen $3.99

Sinclair Smith

☐ MC46126-5 Dream Date $3.99
☐ MC45063-8 The Waitress $3.99

Available wherever you buy books, or use this order form.